fagih@hotmail.com

LIBYAN STORIES

Ahmed Fagih compiles thirteen of the short stories he edited during the seventies and eighties, all published in London in a magazine called Azure. Penned by prominent Libyan writers, these stories shed light on the human experience, especially the experience of those people who inhabit the eastern world. Featuring the work of Abdullah Algwiri, Kamel el Maghor, Ali M. Almisrari, Bashir al Hashmi, Khalifa Takbali, Sayed Gaddaf-Addam, Yousif Al Sharif, Ibrahim el Kouni, K. H. Mustafa, M. El Shwihdi, Yusef Guwairi and Ahmed Ibrahim al Fagih himself, the book illustrates a society in great transformation, as modernity meets tradition, and tension between the two opposing value systems rises.

LIBYAN STORIES

TWELVE SHORT STORIES FROM LIBYA

EDITED BY

AHMED FAGIH

Routledge

Taylor & Francis Group

LONDON AND NEW YORK

First published in 2000 by
Kegan Paul International

This edition first published in 2011 by
Routledge
2 Park Square, Milton Park, Abingdon, Oxfordshire OX14 4RN

Simultaneously published in the USA and Canada
by Routledge
711 Third Avenue, New York, NY 10017

First issued in paperback 2016

Routledge is an imprint of the Taylor and Francis Group, an informa business

British Library Cataloguing in Publication Data
A catalogue record for this book is available from the British Library

ISBN 13: 978-1-138-97978-9 (pbk)
ISBN 13: 978-0-7103-0634-0 (hbk)

Publisher's Note
The publisher has gone to great lengths to ensure the quality of this reprint
but points out that some imperfections in the original copies may be
apparent. The publisher has made every effort to contact original copyright
holders and would welcome correspondence from those they have been
unable to trace.

Libyan Stories

Contents

Acknowledgement

Thanks should be directed to *Azure* magazine, which ceased publication in 1984, where all these short stories and the introduction appeared.

Background Notes on Modern Libyan Literature

Ahmed Fagiih

In this introduction I will mainly be concerned with the achievements of modern Libyan literature in the last few decades. This period saw continuous activity, varied styles and means of expression, and the emergence of diverse schools of thought. The literary movement that has thrived since the early fifties had its earliest beginning at the start of this century; but it was stifled in the time immediately following the Italian seaborne onslaught on Libyan shores on 3rd October 1911. The Italian occupation ended what could have been a very promising literary and cultural movement. The start of this movement had been marked by the publication of the first Arabic newspaper in Libya, *Tripolitania 1866*, during the Othman period. The paper was a single sheet. It was later followed by the publication of a more advanced and independent journal published and edited by the prominent Libyan writer and intellectual; Mohamed al-Busairi. It was called 'Al Taraqqi' (progress) and was issued in 1898. There were other journals: *Al Arraqeeb, Al Kashaf, Alasr Alijadeed, Al Mirsad,* and the satirical journal, *Abu Qisha,* so-called after the pen name of its owner and editor. These published news as well as satirical articles, poems, and linguistic and religious studies. There was also a magazine specialising in science called *Arts*. It was the beginning of a literary and cultural revival, taking its cue from the new spirit that was prevailing in the Arab homeland. With Egypt holding the torch; the same spirit made one of Libya's prominent personalities, Suleiman el Baruni, travel, establish his printing press, publish his newspaper *The Muslim Lion*, and print the first Libyan book of verse – a selection of his poems. To quote the Libyan historian Khalifa Talisi, describing the period:

'The country witnessed a literary revival most manifest in classical studies, the publication of a number of newspapers and the emergence of new literary trends influencing and being influenced by the ones that already existed in the east.' He goes on to say, 'As was the case in other Arab countries, the dominant literary form was poetry as well as studies on language and religion.' Unfortunately all this had to come to an abrupt halt. Nothing could better illustrate the loss suffered by cultural life in Libya than the record kept by the National Library that sixteen journals and periodicals which had appeared regularly just before the Italian invasion were all suppressed by the Italians.

The invaders met with a fierce resistance and for the following twenty years the country and its people had to undergo extreme hardship in the attempt to drive out the invading forces. The Italians' behaviour was contrary even to the usual imperialist philosophy and practice, which would leave some marginal outlet for the natives to enjoy a tiny scope for national development and education. The Italians, in their determination to assimilate the whole country to their own, took no chance. Mussolini called the country 'Libya Italiana' and named it the fourth shore – 'Quatro Spora' – as an extension of Italy. They launched a racist physical and cultural war of extermination. No schools were built for the Libyans, and places of education were limited to mosques, Quranic circles, or the schools of handicrafts which were established during the Ottoman period. The few papers that appeared in these thirty years ceased publication as soon as they came out. Amongst these ill-fated journals was *Alluwa al-Tarabulsi* edited by Othman Qizani, which lent voice to the Libyan people's aspirations. However three other journals managed to continue, they were Abdulla Banoun's *Aladl*, Mahmoud bin Moussa's *Alrageeb Alateed,* and Awad Abinghila's *Al Wattan* (which appeared in Benghazi). The only Arabic magazine which dedicated some pages to new forms of literature like the short story was the monthly *Illustrated Libya*, first published in 1935, under the supervision of the Italian administration. Poetry was the main champion during this period of struggle. The poet Suleiman Albarani was one of the leaders of the liberation war, yet he found time to write poetry and to publish in other Arab countries.

He continued to fight and write until he died in exile in India in 1940. Another poet that the Italians felt was dangerous to their rule was Rafiq al-Muhdawi. They banished him from his country; then he wrote his epic poem, 'Our separation is so painful. Farewell my redeemed land'. He lived in exile in Istanbul and never came back until the Italians left Libya. Ahmed al Sharif was another major literary figure of the period. He was a poet of great potential. He was also a scholar in Islamic law, serving as Judge in the Islamic courts. He had to go through difficult times himself, and wrote a poem urging people to fight.

You can take away our lives
Before our times are up

But there is no way you can take away our pride!

The poet Al Usta Omar joined the ranks of the resistance. His poetry was directly inspired by close involvement with the battlefield. Poets like Ahmed Qunaba and Alfagi Hassan tried to arouse the fighting spirit of the people with their poems and by founding cultural clubs that were subject to closure and other repressive measures. Naturally enough most of the poets concentrated on the message they meant to convey to their oppressed people. The cause was all-important to them. Artistic treatment and style were set aside or considered of secondary importance. Theirs was a direct, militant poetry, whose effect subsided with the occasion that inspired it. But it was exactly this and nothing else that it sought. This poetry was intended as political agitation arousing national fervour, and alerting the people to the atrocities committed by the colonialists. Another understandable reason for the poets' sacrifice of artistic perfection was the intellectual level of their readers, who were genuine in their feelings and original in their attitudes to life, but who were denied the simplest means of education and cultural knowledge. The poet had to relegate highly polished writings to a secondary place. Nevertheless, there are a few examples showing clearly that Libyan poets were capable of attaining a high degree of artistic achievement. Some of Rafiq's love poems are a good indication of this. But the real role was reserved for oral literature and vernacular poetry. Here was a true register of the people's emotions and the battles they fought, and it still lives with us. An example is the poem beginning,

The elderly horseman
Who rides away
Through the fields of fire

Another poem describes the place where the Libyan fighters used to meet:

Blessed is the tent
That has become
Our meeting place

Another tells of the concentration camps that were built by the Italians in the Alagiela area:

I have no illnesses
But the illness of that
Concentration camp

When in 1949 the United Nations recognised the Libyan people's right to independence – which was declared two years later – it was, for the Libyans, the end of nightmares of tyranny, oppression, and coercion. The people were poor beyond comprehension, had scarcely any education and only very primitive and backward means of production. At the time, Libya was described by the United Nations as the poorest of all countries. The people were to wait until 1947 to get their first secondary schools, and till 1956 for their first university to be established. Against this historical background and in the face of such social and cultural circumstances the pioneering writers of the modern era started to found a new literary movement. The post-war era witnessed the homecoming of Libyans living abroad. This was in the late forties, when an active political movement was growing, creating a fresh climate for debates and controversies. Many newspapers appeared, representing different lines of thought, and alongside them, literary trends and particularly the Libyan poetry movement, which welcomed and echoed the poetry schools in the eastern part of the Arab world. Some of the new voices in poetry were Ali Sidgi with his book of free poetry, *Dreams and Revolutions*, Ali Raque with a collection called *Thirsty Nostalgia*, Khalid Zaghbia with *The Great Wall*, Hassan Saleh with *After the War*. They all adopted the new school of poetry, dropping rhymes and keeping the music and the rhythm. Their enthusiasm for modern trends matched their deep awareness of social issues and concern for the poor and downtrodden. The poets identified themselves with their causes, were in constant conflict with the ruling cliques of the time, expressing their patriotic feeling and voicing what the ordinary people felt against the neo-colonist forces that were invading the country in the form of military bases. It was a poetry that was very much influenced by the school of social realism so popular amongst Arab writers of the time, who took their example from social poets with a universal appeal and worldwide reputation – Aragon, Neruda, Nazim Hikmet, and Auden – and who took their lead from Arab poets such as Nazik Almalaika, Al Sayab, Albayati, and the younger poets just making their impact through the well-known Lebanese literary magazine *Al Adab*: Salah Abdul Saboor, Al Fituro, and others. It was natural that the social and political issues of their country should take precedence in their world outlook and their vision for it was harmonious with their cultural and educational background.

The short story, a from newly introduced to the literary scene in Libya, proved a suitable and convenient medium to express the anger and grievances of the writers and to convey their strong indignation against a backward and unjust social system. The most able and accomplished of them was a young lawyer who was educated in Cairo and influenced by the cultural movement there, where the literary page of the *Almisri* newspaper played a leading role. It was edited by writers renowned for their socialist commitment, such as Abdul Rahman al Khamisi and Abdulrahman Alshirgawi. El Maghor returned to become the undisputed pioneer of the realistic story when he wrote tales with very heavy social content at no cost to artistic form. The Romantic school succeeded to a lesser degree and for a shorter time through its spokesman, story writer Abdul Kader Abu Harros. In 1957 he published a collection of short stories under the title *Restless Souls*. They were about emotional frustration and socially imposed separation between men and women. His colleague in the battle for Romanticism was Farid Syala, who published in the same year his book about women's liberation under the title *Towards a Brighter Day to Come* and a sentimental novel, *Confessions of a Human Being*.

The same decade saw the tireless efforts of many Libyan intellectuals to establish the Islamic and Arabic identity of the country which the Italian colonialists had tried in vain to bury. Significant contributions were made by people like Ali Khushaim and Ali Mustafa Almisrati, in his books *Literary Glimpses from Libya, Libyan Journalism in Half a Century*, and his biographies of Libyan freedom fighters such as Khoma, Sadoon, and literary figures such as Al Sharif, Alusta Umor and others. Another colleague of Ali Almisrati is Abdulla Algwiri, who wrote a play about Omar Mukhtar, and another book called *The Meaning of Being*, reflections on the nature of Libyan society.

Historians also assisted in the new revival of national heritage. Sheikh Taher el-Zawi with his books *Heroic Struggle* and *The Country's Chronicles*, and other historical studies, written by Mohammed bin Masoud, Mohammet Bazama and Mustapha Bayou, helped to make up for a serious shortage of studies about Libyan personalities and characteristics. As for literary criticism, prominent among critics was Khalifa Al Talisi who began publishing in 1948, identifying himself with the modern school in literary criticism of which Mohammed Mandour, Maroun Abbod, and Ehsan Abbas were the front runners. Equipped with the knowledge of two foreign languages – Italian and English – an understanding of the works of other nations, as well as a good knowledge of heritage of Arabic literature, Talisi was able to reflect the spirit of the new era when he started to publish his critique of the Libyan writings, his studies of Arabic literature such as that comparing Al Shabby and Yibran, and his book on Rafiq, *The Poet of the Nation*.

The newspapers and reviews of the day lent their pages for the publication of creative writings and cultural debates. Among the central issues on the platform was commitment in arts and literature. Such discussions appeared in papers like *Al Raed, Fazzan, Trapolous Alqarb*. Other debates widely argued in the fifties were classical verse versus free verse, and the use of the vernacular in written dialogue of stories, plays and novels. These discussions reflected a movement seeking its proper direction and increasing its power of perception. Most such activities at the time were attempts to imitate or echo what was happening in the eastern part of the Arab world, particularly Egypt; and whenever a topic became a matter of public debate in these countries, it normally found a place in the Libyan press, with the people taking sides. Every prominent writer would have his imitators and followers inside the country.

The whole literary movement was geared towards the great search for its own identity, for a season of harvest and blossom beyond the horizon. This imitation was yet more apparent in other arts – music, acting, singing. Although this temporal classification has its restrictions and limitations we can still say that as the fifties approached their end, a more vigorous era was about to be ushered in; the overall picture became clearer; writers who before had spoken with the same voice now did their best to speak each in his own unique voice. Direct influence started to disappear; new visions were handled with more accomplished modes of expression; plays, philosophical problems, made their impact.

But the greatest transformation was yet to come; namely, the effects of the oil revenues, which started to pour in in the early sixties. The whole nature of Libyan society began to change, and the cultural impetus had to shift direction and modify its structure. A new reality brought new questions and anxieties. The familiar poverty receded, prosperity although not completely universal changed considerably the standards of living. But the social and cultural upheaval that came with the oil discovery had had its bitter aftermath and brought some negative phenomena, that writers could not ignore; issues such as authenticity in the face of new modernisation, the cultural assimilation, as well as a strong sense of local identity, were evoked, to help resist the invading values of the commercial and consumer society.

The feeling grew that the new wealth, which should be the common property of all the people, was controlled by powers that were alien to the peoples' aspirations and ambitions. Italian merchants were the most active in commerce, the Italian community had a near-monopoly of agriculture, and the foreign banks enjoyed a free hand with no surveillance imposed on them by the Libyan government. Libyan workers were exploited by oil companies, and the American and British military bases were active in maintaining the status quo. All of this contributed to a feeling of bitterness that was reflected in Libyan literature of the sixties. The mood of that era is very well reflected in some of the poems by Ali al Ragai who died on 23rd November 1966. He says in a poem entitled 'Flameless Candles':

What can rain do to barren land
Only the thorns of these cursed cactus
Spreading over the land
I wish these blindfolded eyes could desire to see the light of day
I wish these blindfolded eyes could cry
Could sing
Could suffer
I wish it could remove the mask
Who could open the door
That leads to the fertile land
O ... canary
Who could protect us from the vanity of false desires
And from the agony of barrenness
Before the rust overwhelms our soul
Who could rekindle the flames of passion
Within ourselves and bring forth the melody
Of the coming spring
And close the doors
Against this barbaric wind
O generations of flameless
And thirsty candles
Who will rekindle the flames
Of passion within
Before this rust overwhelms souls.

A vein of political anxiety runs deep into most of the literary creations of the period. This anxiety can be gathered from a review of the titles that were published at the time. *Rebellion* is the collection of short stories by the late Khalifa Takbali. The title story tells of a Libyan worker defying his American boss. *The Wall* by Yousif Al Sharif, dwells lengthily on the wall that was erected ever higher and higher between people, and describes the growth of class distinction, and the unfair distribution of the newly acquired wealth. *Sorrows of Uncle Dokali* by Bashir al-Hashmi tries to capture the ordinary people's daily preoccupation with their livelihood. *Handful of Ashes* and *The Torn Sail* by Ali Misrati are about the frustrations and disappointments people experience every day. *The Yesterday that was Strangled* by Kamel el Maghor refers to the collapse of the old political system and voices hope for a better and more just alternative. To give more telling examples, a play by Abdullah Algwiri, *The Voice and the Echo*, is a premonition of an impending catastrophe which will take place unless rescue arrives.

Another important aspect of the literature of the sixties was undoubtedly the Arab defeat of June 1967, which was to stamp writers with pessimism and dark visions and bitterness. Such was the situation when in 1969 the revolution came to overthrow all those powers which had taken control of society, and to confirm the Arabic and Islamic character of the country, liberating it from the remnants of the colonial power represented by the military bases and foreign influence, and meeting many of the demands of Libyan writers. Short story writer Bashir al-Hashmi talking about pre-Revolutionary literature, says: 'The literary output before the revolution represents a social document much aware of life then. It is a document full of signs telling in its condemnation of the past, dying regime.' The revolution was to transform society radically and to put it in the forefront of our age. The literary scene in the seventies was to witness the first Writers Conference, and the first grouping of writers in the Union of Authors and Writers, later to be called the Authors' and Artists' Association. The seventies also witnessed the founding of a number of publishing houses subsidised by the state, such as the General Establishment for Publishing and the Arab Books House. Before the revolution, publishing was in the hands of the private sector, where the state gives no support. With the public sector helping and encouraging the publication of new writing, books are now being published in large numbers. The circle of writers enlarges year after year. Newcomers are constantly arriving with original offerings and a fresher outlook. The striking feature of the creative works written in this period, as Mohamed Al Zawi, was the emergence of the intellectual as a major character. There are two reasons for this phenomenon. First, the wide programme of education. The educated man became an integral part of society and not, as in previous times, an invisible minority. Second, the emergence of new intellectual and philosophical preoccupations in the minds of our writers. These are so deep and complex that writers cannot just put them into the mouths of the old type characters which were in most cases workers or village people.

This has been a very quick look at the background of modern Libyan literature which, in turn, is only a small part of the shade and colour of the vast and rich panorama of modern Arabic literature.

1

The Oil and the Dates
Abdullah Algwiri

He felt his blood boil, a hot pulse coursed through his veins, his heart was pounding against his chest. The window pane was cracked and the paint was peeling off the walls. The sun had not yet set, the smell of something stale emanated from a far corner of the room. The rickety wooden box on which he sat shook. There was a hole in the side of his shoe. He had not slept a wink last night, nor had he eaten anything since the previous evening. His guts twisted and a muffled rumbling reached his ears. He'd been thinking but he wouldn't say anything yet. He will leave time to resolve the matter, but what was the solution? He had no idea. He had considered all aspects of the problem last evening but had reached no conclusion. He will have to leave things alone, it was no good.

The water he had left in the pot boiled in the kitchen. The smell of onions filled his hands. The aroma of fried garlic coming from some neighbour pervaded the air, but there was nobody to call out to. His father had died and left him – and had also bequeathed him other thing to torment him. The days stretched as long as the minaret. He sometimes compared the length of the minaret with that of the oil-press chimney. The well in the orchard had dried up and was useless. The olive trees had not borne any fruit last year. The dates had not been gathered from the palm trees. He searched a long time for someone to gather the dates but without success. He had gone to look for the date gatherer he knew but was told:

'He has gone to live in the city.'

So he asked:

'What's he doing in the city? There are no palm trees there.'

They answered him:

'He's working as a watchman.'

He enquired:

'So who gathers the dates then?'

'No one.'

He remembered the olives but hesitated before asking. One of the men, as if reading his thoughts, said:

'Not even the olives! You won't find anybody to gather them.'

Another laughed and added:

'You won't find anyone, even if you offer to share the yield with them.'

Dust particles invaded his nostrils. One of the men was holding a donkey by its collar. The bleating of sheep filled the air. Suddenly an unexpected silence fell everywhere, to be interrupted by the braying of a donkey. Green pieces of paper emerged from pockets and were exchanged by several hands. The man standing next to him was being obstinate, he insisted then refused. Hands continued to stretch out towards him.

The man shouted:

'I shan't sell him at that price!'

The man standing opposite him asked:

'His price? For God's sake, what's his price?'

Several words mingled in front of him and he could not distinguish between them. He didn't know why he remained standing there. He didn't realise how he got to be involved in the dispute. He nodded his head a few times and he smiled once. His thoughts strayed for a few seconds but he remained standing, wanting to ask once more about a date or olive harvester. It was the first time that he had to handle these matters. The argument going on around him was concerning the price of a ram. He heard the man standing next to him say:

'It's not just his price. Look at him! Just you try and lift him off the ground ...if it wasn't for necessity, I wouldn't sell him. I was going to keep him for the feast. I chose him out of a whole flock. You couldn't find such rare meat in all the market.'

The man standing opposite still asked:

'His price? By God, what's his price?'

He moved forward as if to examine the ram but realised how ridiculous that would be. What did he care about the ram? He measured his steps as he moved away and left the market behind him. The shouts of the seller and the buyer grew fainter until they left no trace on his mind.

The smell of the blazing sand baking under the scorching sun rose above his head. He could discern his house in the distance. His mother will be asking him about the dates and the olives. She was as prudent about their means of living as his father was. He will have to tell her that he could not find the date gatherer or anybody else. She will no doubt utter words of mournful regret about his father and volunteer to undertake the business in hand herself. Yes, he knew that she would have liked to supervise the work in their orchard, she could not neglect their livelihood and she will taunt him because he could not do the job. Her words about their 'livelihood' will wound his ears, and his mother would ask for the hundredth time:

'Do I have to go out and look for someone to take care of the orchard?'

He will answer:

'No.'

'What then? Are we going to neglect our livelihood?'

'My salary will suffice.'

'But what about the oil and the dates? Our whole stock for the year?!'

'We'll buy some from the market.'

'When we already have an orchard!'

'Well, what's to be done?'

'What's to be done? Hasn't your father told you ...'

He will lose his temper and interrupt her irritably:

'Everybody buys from the market!'

She would then bemoan her misfortune and curse her fate, and perhaps curse him. She would cry in anguish and remember the times when his father was alive ... she will remember everything to the day ... she will recall many things about him ... about his work. He will just have to submit to all this quietly. He won't say a word.

He stumbled on the front doorstep. He heard a loud voice, then his mother's voice, mingled with crying and moaning. They faced each other. He felt his blood boiling and a hot pulse rushed through his veins. His heart beat wildly against his rib cage.

He asked him:

'My brother ... what's happened?'

After the brother calmed down a bit, he muttered something and turned his head away.

He replied in controlled tones:

'Nothing.'

'Nothing? How? What's the matter?'

His brother's voice rose a little:

'I've told you ... it's nothing.'

'I've got eyes!'

'God forbid ... I've told you it's nothing.'

'Praise be to God.'

He remained quiet for a while, then he addressed the question to his mother. Tears were coursing silently down her cheeks. Her eyes fixed on his face.

'Mother ... what's up?'

She said nothing but a sob shook her body. He turned to his

brother and asked:

'Aren't you going to tell me ...?'

A minute passed, sharp as a knife, the passing seconds nearly severing his nerves. The pane of glass in the only small window in the room was cracked, bit of paint have been peeling off the walls. His brother turned to him suddenly and said in a low voice, with his head hanging down:

'I told her ... I'm selling my share.'

His eyes opened wide but without a glimmer. He held his breath for a long while then exhaled it forcibly:

'You're selling your share?!'

'Yes.'

The trace of a smile appeared on his lips, he hesitantly moved towards his brother and whispered:

'You've frightened her, my brother.'

His brother replied quickly:

'I meant what I said.'

'You meant what you said! You really mean it ... you mean you really mean it!'

'I said I'm going to sell my share ... it's my right and it's my inheritance.'

'But this is our livelihood ... my brother.'

'I'm selling my share!'

The sun still scorched the ground. The stale smell still crept from the room and pervaded his nostrils, damp and clammy. His eyes fell on the wooden box.

After a pause he said:

'Do you want people to laugh at us?'

His brother asked sharply:

'People laugh? At what?'

'At what you intend to do.'

'That's a good one! If I choose to sell my share of the land ... people would laugh!'

'Yes ... we must increase it, not sell it.'

'Well, I'm selling.'

There was a hole in the side of his shoe. Last night he hadn't slept a wink.

'I was thinking. I shall start repairing the house again.'

'Think as you please. As for me, I'm selling.'

'What's the hurry?'

'I was offered a good price.'

'Have you offered it for sale already?'

'Yes.'

'So ... you've been thinking of selling for a long time!'

'I want to live in the city.'

'We can all live in the city ... but we mustn't sell.'

'I want the money ... I want to live like other people!'

He had not eaten anything since yesterday. His guts twisted and inner rumblings reached his ears.

'Let me think about it.'

'What do I care. Think or don't think. The city keeps expanding ... the land's value is increasing ... who'd have thought the orchard would be measured in metres?'

'Let me think.'

'And who's stopping you from thinking ... you're strange!'

He thought ... but he didn't say anything ... He would just have to leave time to solve the problem ... but what was the solution? He had no idea. There was no longer a smell of garlic in the air, the smell of onions had disappeared from his hands. He wished she would shout at him. Their eyes met suddenly and he heard his brother say:

'We must divide the orchard.'

He turned towards his mother. She sometimes 'died' in instants. He recalled the length of the minaret which their neighbour had built for the mosque which their father had set up ... and compared it with the chimney of the oil press. He heard his brother say quietly:

'Don't let's fall out. The Sheikh at the mosque will divide our shares. The well has dried in the orchard, it's of no use. The olive trees didn't yield last year. There's nobody to gather the dates. I've met our brother-in-law. I've asked him to represent our sister at the sharing out.'

The date gatherer was now a watchman in the city. They could not find anybody to gather the olives, even on the basis of going halves with them. The ram's price was too high, but the purchaser wanted to buy him at any price, still the owner refuses, swearing by its virtues and boasting about its merits. The bleating of a goat could be heard from inside the house. He had bought it two months ago for his mother to add to the two calves which still remained after his father's funeral. His brother's words stuck in his mind. He dwelt on all these matters but could not reach a solution. Is he to leave everything? It was no use. The old woman huddled there, her head bowed. Suddenly he blurted out:

'I won't sell him at that price!'

His brother was puzzled:

'Sell what?'

'The ram.'

His brother's eyes opened wide in bewilderment. Astonishment parted his lips open and filled the space within.

'What ram?'

'Indeed what ram?'

'Didn't you say that you wouldn't sell him at that price?!'

He hung his head and said nothing. The brother asked:

'You mean you won't sell your share? You're free to do as you please.'

His mother did not ask him who would look after the orchard, nor did he ask about their livelihood which his father had secured for them. It was he who asked:

'But the oil and the dates and the yearly stock!'

His brother laughed and moved closer to him. He placed his hand on his shoulder and said in slow, quiet, deliberate tones:

'Everything's in the market, oil and dates and confectioneries and almonds.'

He didn't question him any more. His mother did not ask who was going to work in the orchard. His salary will suffice. His mother kept quiet and didn't utter a word. He made no reference to what he expected of her, but looked kindly at her. She lifted her head and he saw in her eyes words she did not wish to voice. He said to himself: 'Such is the state of the world … separations.'

His voice rose in spite of himself and he muttered his thoughts:

'God curse the devil!'

His mother, too, uttered something but he couldn't make it out. As he moved to leave his brother's voice followed him:

'We'll meet this evening … The Sheikh is coming, so is our brother-in-law. The sun hasn't set yet.'

His foot stumbled on the floor of the room. A blast of hot dry air engulfed him. His blood was still boiling and his heartbeats throbbed rhythmically in his chest.

2

Crying
Kamel el Maghor

Omran never cried, as he cried that day; his tears got mixed with the grains of sand, and made his face look like a patch of old freckles ... His eyes were exploring the high new buildings, and their balconies, from behind a screen of dust, looked down at the people. A new road was being made, and hundreds of eyes were following the bulldozer, its wide jaws eating up walls one after the other. Its triangular teeth hauled stones and bricks with ecstasy ... pieces of building material were scattered around like the saliva of a child when he chews a piece of chocolate. Its wheels were just like giant legs striding along with determination, it was a one-eyed monster, a big hole of an eye in the front burning with light as it watched its mouth engulfing falling walls and stamping them with its feet. It was opening up a wide road for new high buildings to be erected, with balconies to look down at people walking with sad tearless eyes, moving heavily. Omran was crying, shedding tears as he never did before, his eyes were wide open as he looked up across the door with that dishevelled hair of his, the grains of sand sticking to his face, specks getting into his eyes and making him blink. He heard the bulldozer's footsteps, its teeth ate the road (Omran's road) piece by piece. When he first heard it he was taken aback. He felt it coming, its wheels touching the earth and leaving behind a scream – like rumbling.

He held his school-books to his chest, his eyes narrowed as he watched the giant machine coming nearer to one of the houses with solid white walls which proudly stood up trying to resist. The wall seemed inexhaustible with a green door in the middle, the lock yellow, and it was shining under an early day sun. The machine teeth came nearer and Omran was closely watching, he was now standing at the entrance witnessing the clash. The whiteness of the wall invaded Omran's eyes which grew larger, and it seemed to him that the wall became wider, its shadow broader than the road where the people sit to whisper together in the shadow as night falls. Some of them, relaxing there, would take the machine lightly, go about or relieve themselves or do necessary chores as darkness prevailed on the road wider and larger than the machine ... wider than its cabin and the tiny man who sits in it and surveys the wall surface. The machine, when Omran first saw it, was no more than a small toy, the like of which they gave to him on feast days. It used to move in the road just like a toy of his, it would move forward towards the wall, touch it, and then it would stop, probably out of order, or broken, but it would not go through the wall. Until this day, until that moment, Omran was watching the game with joy, for he knew that the wall would resist the machine; the bulldozer's teeth would fall out just like the teeth of an old man who was trying to chew a bone. And when the machine stopped after a few jerks, the smoke filtering up, and there was a mechanical screech, Omran was greatly disappointed, his big toy seemed to have run out of steam, no power left in it. He saw the short man, his head coming out of the steering cabin, seeking help from the onlookers, and begging them to reconstruct it. The wall ahead was wide and white ... its green door was smiling ... Omran, now, wished the machine to continue working until it would reach the wall, heading into a crash, then he would see it stop, with its teeth broken, and its front smashed. His eyes were on the lookout, silence reigned supreme round the machine, its smoke got mixed with the dust and gave it its own colouring. Omran then thought differently, that the toy should not be his great love for the great wall and its cheering colour ... for it did not normally stand still, but, like this, gave few jerks, was loud for a bit, and then lost power again, the driver asking people to repair it. Omran's eyes questioned the faces of the people round the machine and he had the feeling that they did not comprehend the toy, they were still, senseless, for them there was no sudden revelation; and even when the machine stirred again before it stopped they were passively watching its wheels as if to urge it to pick itself up and get moving. They seemed to be fed up with the game. The way they stood there reminded him of young schoolboys watching a naughty colleague being punished by the schoolteacher during the break. The machine could hardly be heard. The people's collective gaze lay in the shadow of the white wall, the silvery glow of the door handle. The tiny man dared to look out of the cabin, then disappeared inside again as if silence horrified him. The moment of expectation lengthened in Omran's mind, it was as if he must be as attentive as when taking care not to miss the bell announcing the beginning of the school class. The machine was continuously shaking. The spouts of smoke from its top sounded like an old woman's coughs.

The wall was always the same, its shadow changed its position so heavily that it was hardly noticeable. No one was sitting in the shade, it was unbothered by the machine. The wall's shadow was utterly defensive; in contrast to the bulldozer, it produced no smoke and got no man on top of it to urge people to help it out of its ordeal, its only power it derived from the wall itself which extended from the entrance of the alleyway up to the house lying next to it. People didn't seem to look at it ... their sad eyes were following the machine's movements, their noses inhaled smoke and the lobes of their ears seemed to have grown longer. They were sad and taciturn, a defeated football team awaiting the end of the match ... And all of a sudden the voice of the machine started to be regular. The sporadic smoke turned into a very black and thick rope. The wheels took on a determined forward movement, making the people round beat a retreat muttering to themselves. The machine was determinedly moving forward, lifting its teeth in the air and coming down again, then it opened the jaws and moved on and on. When it had almost reached the wall, Omran filled his lungs with air, stopped breathing and clutched his school exercise books firmly. He didn't wait long before he saw the shadow giving way, the yellowish silver handle of the door was no more shiny. It was as if the machine was walking heavily on his heart among dust and smoke.

And it was not long before he saw the courtyard of the house with its remaining three walls and the interior of the rooms and their green doors. The remaining walls were full of cracks and splinters just like his agonised heart ... his eyes were shedding tears mixing them with sand so that his face looked like a patch of old freckles. He could not distinguish people's eyes. They were hidden behind a smokescreen of dust, their voices could not be heard. They were lost in the ensuing fall of masses of bricks on the floor. Were they trying to hold back their tears? As for Omran he never cried as he cried that same day and later on when he was sitting on his seat in the class the picture of the bulldozer wiping out walls one after another constantly came to his mind. He saw the bulldozer's teeth biting the shop of Abeed the greengrocer, dispersing lots of vegetables, like blood, he saw it eating up the house of Al Sadiq, leaving it open for the prying eyes of men and women, he then saw the heavy, heavy steps taking a heavy toll at a hut, dismantling it, and the hens running away from their cages, the kids chasing them. The whole road was eventually turned into a wasteland for the kids to play football in it while the Italians looked down from the tops of the balconies at the undisciplined kids chased by policemen.

He was never as eloquent as he was that day. In his own words the machine was his staunch and sole enemy. To his classmate sitting next to him he said:

'Big, big, as big as a high building.'

His eyes visualised the pain caused by the movement of the machine as if it was walking on their chests, and what made it the more painful was that its victims did not nudge or stir, and the toy was no more a toy, no wall can withstand it, not even the double layered wall of the school, nor the headmaster's room. He told the students all about it while they were having their breakfast.

'It was like a train and as noisy.'

His way of describing it reached sometimes ecstatic and rhapsodic pitch as if it was a feast for the eyes. He made them relive what he saw by acting with movements and gestures the way the machine was pounding and moving walls and he was so absorbing that they moved aside to let him, the machine pass.

The only difference was that he had two eyes while it had just one, and his two eyes were drenched with tears. He tried to make his hatred of the machine contagious to arouse in them the same deep resentment, and even to stop them being curious about it. Their curiosity he wished to transform into clear drops of tears, sharing with him the same lament for the walls and hatred for the machine. Its teeth were like an elephant, he said. A unanimous apprehension prevailed. He still could smell the smoke, its noise was still louder than the noise in the class and the teacher's lecture. Its one and only eye was looking at him, following him. Its arm trying to reach, to eat him up just like it did with the walls. It frightened grown-ups as well. Omran was never frightened as he was making his way home, his heavy steps were trying to avoid the machine tracks ... the roads were no more straight and lined with houses. They were like a courtyard full of skeletons of houses scattered round. The high buildings' balconies were like eyes supervising him stealing his way home. He was hoping desperately not to meet the machine's eye and let it spot him, use him for a frightful spree. To open up its teeth, crack his bones and silence the crying of his eyes. The road was deserted and silent. The walls reflected no shadows, no brass door handle shone. No bustling in the midday market-place and when Omran approached Al Haja's hut he saw the yellow machine. It was put away and under its wheels there were patches of sticky black liquid and there was no smoke coming out of the spout. No light in the front. Its long arm was immobile and horizontal as if it were a man in a sleeping position. Its two jaws were locked and lazily dangling, and some bricks and sand could be seen between the teeth.

A serpentine shadow could be seen lying to the right of the

machine, a man could be seen sitting there, with the tea kit in front of him, making tea as skilfully as others.

The nearer he got the more his fears grew, of the machine spotting him, moving its sleeping arm, rekindling the flame in its one and only eye and the man lying in its shadow to jump, stuff himself into the cabin and set it working to crush his bones. His fears were sweat drops growing in numbers and running down his legs, paralysing him. The machine's shadow was betraying an immense curiosity inviting him to come nearer to the man with the tea kit. His eyes continued to watch the machine and the machine's shadow would frighten him, equally, should it move, making the machine a shadowless monster. Incessantly he watched with his eyes on its dormant arm, the soily area round its wheels similar to the heaps of dust surrounding the cemetery, as he gathered the sound of oil drops from the fuel tank, reminding him of a loose water tap.

Omran's life will never witness an action-packed day as that day. He was moving, moving, towards the machine, tears receding to the folds of his heart, his steps growing wider and wider. Every time he felt the oil drops sticking to the black sweat pond underneath, he would closely hug his exercise books ... but the distance between them was not disappearing. It persisted since it was made of fear, hatred and curiosity. He imagined the machine attacking walls one after another, pulling them down, but finally he found himself face to face with it; his wide-open eyes confronting the glassy, extinguished eye. He shook his head, and put his hands in front of his face and moved closer. He was sweating, and trying to resist an urgent desire to urinate. As if to attack it he made a shrilling noise, he shook himself again and touched her with two fingers. He felt the sun's heat running through its iron body and shrank back ... his eyes facing its one and only eye, he put out his arm and tried to climb it. It was still inaccessible, possibly it was asleep, a big toy that does not feel the fumblings of the tiny. He started to turn round it many times, his feet stumbled on its sticky dark sweat. He saw its breathing pipe.

And when he touched again the iron of its legs he did not feel any fear. He suddenly felt that it was a mere toy, a big toy though, that can breath and sweat. It was only when the short man sat inside its cabin and switched it on that it could move between houses and eat walls, and make road extensions of uninhabitable lands.

He attacked it, but it did not attack back, he angrily opened his eyes to the maximum he could; it did not open its eye. He clenched his fist in defiance but it did not budge or respond. He then moved back and with all the power he could muster he kicked it on the face with his foot. Despite the pain he felt, he did not really enjoy the thrill of vengeance. He felt nothing as the bulldozer iron stood there motionlessly while he was agonising in silence with the terrible pain in his toes. Tears streamed down Omran's cheeks as they had never streamed before. His tears were touched by the air in the uninhabitable land and making a screen of fog to blur his vision for a while. He then took to the road and with slow painful legs he continued walking and looking for his home.

3

An Extract from Mussolini's Nail
Ali M Almisrati

Fara'as was in his shop, rather than seeing il Duce's procession he wished a car would run over him or the earth would break and engulf him. And during those days of strife he used to get the bulletins and newspapers issue by Balbu's bureau. He would call his children to come inside the house, and lock the doors and the window shutters.

Then he would spit on il Duce and the ruler's pictures, tear them up and throw them in the fireplace.

He would then say to his children:

'This is your enemy. Italy requisitioned our property, it set up nooses, and killed your grandfather and your cousin.'

Fara'as father fell victim in 'Alhani' battle, his brothers in that of 'Al-Sahil'.

Fara'as wound was so deep it could not be healed. He would tell his sons, with tears welling up in his eyes, that the ritual of spitting on and burning of the pictures should be a secret, and that nothing of what he said at home should go outside the confines of the house.

One day his younger son came home to tell him about the latest song they had learned in school:

'Rome, we shall be faithful to you.' Impulsively he gave his son a smack, then, to make up for this cruel gesture he hurried to hug him, wipe away his tears and apologise:

'My son, the Italians are our enemies, they killed your grandfather and with their bullets they wiped out your cousins.'

The son then memorised the original ballad of the strugglers with the encouragement of his father who eventually asked him to keep it for himself and not to sing it in public.

Fara'as then went to the doctor to ask him to give his son permission to stay home for medical reasons. This way his son would not take part in the procession celebrating the arrival of il Duce, along with thousands of other poor youngsters.

He was in his shop again, thinking how days run fast, as fast as snakes, the day il Duce is due to arrive is unbelievably near, a nightmare was depressing his heart.

Many times he thought of emigration, to follow in the steps of

23

thousands of his own desert people. They managed to leave just before the Italians gained control of the borders. But what about his wife and children? Must he run away and leave them behind?

Many years of his life he spent in jail. Bitter and torturous years they were and when he was at last set free, he found that the Italians had expropriated his property and his means of livelihood.

He then decided to start afresh by making Arabic horse-saddles, but it was not all sweet and honey; he had his share of wretchedness and misery.

Fara'as was an artist who lavished all his skills on making elegant Arabic horse-saddles. He chose the best of leathers and thongs, and on a shelf in the shop he kept the saddle most dear to him. It was the saddle on which his father fought the *jihad*, a bullet-hole around which were dry spatters of glorious blood still there to remind him of the dear past.

The story of the saddle is folded deep in his heart. He recounts it only to the best of friends, and Fara'as used to look at it every day, sometimes daring to touch it gently, silently.

His sons he thought, when they grow up should go and live in another Arab country, to breathe air uncontaminated by the Fascists, their heavy boots and their hunting dogs.

He mastered making saddles and decorating them, through experience and by previously attending the Islamic Arts and Handiwork's School. The saddles he loved to make, thinking of horsemen, those struggling desert-dwellers and their battles.

Unfortunately they are no more to be found.

The *jihad* battles were the end of them; their spring of chivalry and heroism is over. Instead it was the Fascists' turn to admire his masterful elegant craftsmanship and artistic accomplishment.

Things turned sour, for he bitterly resented those Italians coming to his shop to admire his ornamented and perfect art.

But he had to accept selling saddles to them. Survival was at stake. Dark memories haunted him, and the only outlet of light and hope was a graceful sheikh who lectured in a mosque. Most of the evenings he went to the mosque to sit by and listen to what the glorious sheikh said. He was sweet-tongued, his clear eyes showed intelligence, his voice was mild and affectionate.

Sometimes, the sheikh would come to the shop, take a small seat in front of the shop. When the two felt there was no eye watching or ear eavesdropping they gave speech to their thoughts.

'When shall their end come, the dark night is getting longer and longer.'

The sheikh would reply in his faithful and bright voice, a voice that was not allowed to be slackened by the years:

'Their end will be the worst of all ends.'

'They want to take Egypt and Tunisia as well.'

'When shall the nightmare be over?'

Calmly the sheikh replied:

'God gives time, but does not completely forget wrongdoers. The fate of il Duce and his followers of hunting dogs will be the worst of all.'

Fara'as then looked at the road and added:

'Darkness is getting longer and heavier. My sons and the sons of my sons will have to grow up under the regime of the Fascist. What kind of life imposed by fate is this life?'

The sheikh replied:

'God is all mercy and justice, states and empires flourished and then perished. Remember the Spaniards, the Vandals, the Maltese, and the despotic Walis. Remember that Tripoli has wiped out all of them. The martyrs' blood will not be wasted.'

Fara'as would then fall silent, at least he felt more content as long as there was a shimmer of light – the light of faith coming in from the window. But it was not long before he said:

'I wish to live just one day in which I would witness the enemy broken and his eviction from the country.'

'Trust in God,' the sheikh replied.

'Il Duce's faith will be the worst of all fates. The end of every traitor will be telling in its consequences. Darkness will lead to light, my son.'

Fara'as was bewildered. At the doorstep of his shop stood one of those gloomy faces he so much hated and never wished to see; it was the face of one of those detectives, who through hypocrisy, managed to be included in Balbu's and Badilo's entourage. He went to Rome several times and accompanied il Duce's procession, licking the tyrants' shoes.

Fara'as had always tried to stop his eyes from meeting those detective's eyes. But here he was, right in front of his shop, walking slowly and brandishing his coloured and ornamented whip, wearing his Roman hat; the renegade speaks Arabic, but he showed off his Italian which he speaks with many flaws and an accent. Seeing him standing there made Fara'as pray in silence.

He then entered the shop and saluted Fara'as coldly through the nose.

Fara'as could not help noticing that his mouth was like the seat of

a dog ridden with scabies. The detective then took his time
contemplating some of the crafts on display.

He then pointed to one of the saddles and asked:

'Is this one of your making?'

The answer was as brief as possible.

'Yes.'

The answer was obviously not to the liking of the detective; he
felt outraged by this workman, who showed no hospitality or
respect. What is this dry and dull behaviour, the dull detective
thought. He then put up his head, the same head he keeps low when
he meets his master and said:

'Are you Fara'as?'

'Yes.'

'I thought I knew you. We have a file in the name of your father.
He was one of the strugglers. He was an Arab who stood against
Italians. Is that not true?'

These words sent a shiver down Fara'as' spine. He saw
immediately in his mind's eye his children, then the noose and the
jail. Are the Italians still after him? Was it not enough for them that
they had already put him in jail and requisitioned his property? But
he managed to keep his composure. Heavy moments of silence
before the detective added:

'It seems to me that you are still lucky. A golden chance is ahead
for you ...'

Fara'as was impatiently waiting with the bodkin in his hand ready
to pierce the bloodshot eyes of this idiot.

Again he managed to control himself.

'You know that il Duce is going to visit Libya.'

Fara'as was recommended to do the saddle for il Duce's horse.
His Excellency the Wali was to present il Duce with the saddle. And
Fara'as the best maker of Arabic saddles was chosen for the honour.
You should rejoice then Fara'as, everybody is happy. But Fara'as
could not bring himself to say anything, a whirlwind was storming
in his head.

'You are lucky, Fara'as,' the detective said, 'the present will be
made by your own hands. It is a great honour for you.'

He looked at the chameleon-faced detective. Should he spit on
him, thus letting off some steam from his boiling chest? His heart-
beat quickened as he tried with difficulty to keep himself under
control. When shall this nightmare end?

The detective then looked around the shop's walls and asked:

'Where is il Duce's picture? Why do you not hang up il Duce's picture?'

The detective seemed to have discovered the noose-rope by which he will hang Fara'as. He shouted and shouted again:

'How come that you do not put up il Duce's picture – il Duce, the leader and the hero of Rome?'

At this point, Fara'as broke his silence, always afraid that his tongue might wrongly translate his inner feelings. He squeezed his hands, looked at the detective and said:

'Every night we celebrate il Duce's picture at home. His picture and that of God are in our heart ...'

Luckily the detective did not know how they celebrated il Duce's picture at home. It is one of God's blessings that the detective did not know. 'Yes, il Duce's picture is in our heart, but it is grooved with hate, and anger.' Fara'as was thinking to himself, 'a picture the strugglers and freedom-fighters will not leave in peace.'

The detective thought that Fara'as' answer was no different from the answers given by the mercenaries and the dupes. He was pleased and nodded his empty head. Meanwhile, Fara'as wished the earth would engulf him rather than leave him alive to witness such an encounter with a person, asking him to make with his own fingers a saddle for a Fascist and a butcher.

The detective then continued:

'You are lucky Fara'as, you have a golden chance.'

He wanted to evade the issue, to run away, but how?

He brooded a while, then an idea came to him:

'Your Excellency might not know that I suffer from some paralysis in my fingers. I cannot, really, do stitching or embroidery.'

'You make me wonder who did all these beautifully ornamented saddles. Everybody is talking about you, the country over, and how come you open the shop day and night if you have paralysis? You must have a grudge in your heart; you still have in you some Arab blood, just like those groups who fled to Tunis and Egypt.'

Fara'as then picked himself up and interrupted the spate of contemptuous words.

'My fingers cannot make a great and beautiful saddle worthy of il Duce, the leader of Italy.'

The detective was not pleased:

'O gracious God, how come that you cannot? The celebrations committee have chosen you for this grand mission. You might not know that even His Highness the Wali and the general registrar have a good mention of your saddles – admired your crafts very much and they were very well received everywhere they were exhibited, in

Rome, Milan and Paris. How can you reject an honour bestowed on you? It seems to me that you are still a block-headed Arab.'

Fara'as replied:

'Look, my fingers are trembling from some months now. I just sell saddles now; I am not making any. Moreover, I am looking for somebody to help me and here you come asking me to make a saddle for il Duce.'

At this point the detective's tone of speech took on a threatening accent:

'No excuses whatsoever! This is an order and we will come back tomorrow to confirm the matter.'

As the detective was turning his head and moving away he asked:

'What is the reason for the trembling anyway?'

'Because of the dampness of the jail.'

'Oh, you must be then one of the struggler Arabs who used to threaten Italy...'

Instinctively Fara'as knew that the conversation was reaching the danger point, as it is no secret that the detective would not have acquired his high grades and would not be among Balbu's entourage if he had not victimised innocent people, fabricated indictments and chased the strugglers' sons. Then he heard the trumpet and the canon. The detective stood still and turned to the side of the street. It was time to salute the tri-coloured flag. As for Fara'as he was still in the shop, mumbling to himself something about an imminent danger, and peering at his martyred father's saddle, fighting against a sweeping desire to take it and hit the idiot's head with it. Fever was running high inside him, a fever that befalls those with injustice done to them.

As the lowering and folding of the flag ceremony ended the detective shouted:

'Come back to your senses, the leader of the land will be honouring the land in no more than a few days. Even His Highness the Wali sits late at night in his office to direct the visit's programme and it is in his name that we order you to make an Arab saddle of the best kind. The Wali himself will drop in to see you for you know His Highness is a modest man and he likes the Arabic market.'

As Fara'as made his way home, he brooded over his dilemma. It was an impasse he should manage to bypass, the son of strugglers as he was. He was a Fascist victim, the colonisers dispersed his family. And must he really make a saddle to be ridden by Mussolini? ...The Italians did not seem to be satisfied with the many saddles they already had. He could not bring himself to sleep.

At night there was an unexpected knock at the door.

A knocking at the doors of the strugglers' houses in the black age of terror could usher in the danger of exile or hanging.

The woman was frightened of the knocking which seemed to go on and on. It was the detective. He was trying to recover his breath and panting, he said:

'This is the first-class leather and the strings to make the saddle in three days ... His Highness the Governor Balbu urges you to be diligent and good.'

Fara'as said nothing. Different kinds of feelings were moving in his head and heart. The detective with his instinct and by the way Fara'as looked, knew that Fara'as was hesitant. An old hand in treachery, the detective said emphatically:

'Mr Fara'as you've a chance here, and you might like to know that I have in my pocket a list of some Arabs. And it won't take more than a few lines with the pencil to have your name added to the list. Then and only then you will find no way out.'

He will carry it out, and let be what be.

He then made the much-coveted saddle and he did it very very well.

But in all secrecy he fixed in it a very sharp nail, automatically set so that it would come up quickly and would bore into the rider and make him bleed. He did not tell anybody about it, and after the finishing touches, he wrapped the saddle carefully.

Every time the detective passed, he would say with a voice, coarsened by shouting, to Fara'as :

'Are you not lucky with this chance at hand? ... I wish it was me who did the saddle, or even a horse cover. The man presenting the cover, from the gentry, will be decorated with an extra grade and will have his picture taken next to the leader.'

Fara'as then would reply with a smile:

'Horse covers are easier than saddles.'

Then the go-ahead was given to the celebration. For two days, from dawn onward, people were forced to gather at certain points in columns and queues.

They brought somebody to present Mussolini with the 'Islam Sword' with shivers and tremblings.

It was general mobilisation and pandemonium in the Fascist army. Then the big surprise came ...

As soon as il Duce sat on the horse, the automatic nail came up and sharply bored him.

He screamed, his face was blood-shot.

Next to him was the Wali Balbu and some Fascist stooges.

But his scream was lost unheard amidst a concert of noise and clapping. The nail made him bleed, but the masses were not aware of anything odd. As il Duce was cursing and feeling around the nail, his henchmen were scurrying around to remedy the situation. They replaced the saddle from another nearby horse.

The crowd thought that il Duce's screams were one of his usual fits of oratory. They continued to clap and jovially repeat his name ...

A few hours later Fara'as was escorted to jail.

No one inquired about his fate, whether it was deep in the sea or sealed by the noose ... But Fara'as in any case was happy with his revenge, for as they were coming to take him to prison for interrogation, he was hugging his father's saddle and kissing the bloodstains on it.

4

Screams in our Village
Bashir al Hashmi

The noise was getting louder and louder. Masses of people, running through the narrow alleys. An atmosphere of fear and horror threw its shadow on everything. Even the land of our village seemed to express its dismay and anger: the wind blew dust, and shook trees, causing a rushing sound which filled the air, intermingling with the other noise. From time to time distinct sounds emerged: children crying, women wailing, dogs barking. The sun's rays struggled, trying to penetrate through clouds of dust. People muttered rebelliously, 'The Italians! The Italians!' An old man who was exhausted from walking leaned on his stick, trying in vain to hold back his incessant coughing, out of breath, looking at the mass of people turned into shadows by a storm of dust. His puzzled mind was mirrored in the wrinkles on his shocked face which seemed to ask,

'What is going on?'

A small child was running, screaming, trying to reach his mother who was holding on to her baby, dragging behind her the hem of her shabby dress which was blowing into the baby's face, blocking his spasmodic screams –

'Mother! Mother!'

A blind old lady was running behind two women crying and wailing,

'My son Soleiman! My son Soleiman!'

She nearly collapsed and the two women rushed to her rescue. They were followed by a group of men pulling donkeys loaded with all the luggage they could carry, old folks, men and women, and little children. A voice came through, much louder than the prevailing noise, crying,

'Salima! Salima!' But Salima was speeding up, slapping her own face, crying, 'Mabrouk! Mabrouk!' A man knelt down and rose up with something in his arms which he rushed to the woman. 'Your son, Salima.' She held the baby but soon collapsed with him in her arms. A number of men rushed to carry her. Voices scattered by the blowing wind:

'Salima, Al Mabrouk fled from the Italians ... Al Mabrouk did

31

not die, don't be frightened. This morning I handed arms to Al Mabrouk together with other fighters.'

From the back a man was running; out of breath he cried,

'The Italians have entered the farms and the houses.'

An old man sitting on a donkey exclaimed loudly,

'Did they find him?'

'No,' was the answer.

'Good,' he replied. Faces suffering from sleeplessness and exhaustion began to smile. Another voice was heard expressing joy at the news.

Another wave of men rushed through from everywhere making more noise.

'The Italians are coming after us. They are looking for their captain. It's over. The captain was kidnapped and killed.' An old man raised his hand shouting,

'Their captain is not worth the bag of pepper I've lost.'

From afar another group of men were hailing and shouting,

'The Italians are in front of you, as well as behind you ... stop, everyone!'

They slowed down while another group of people stopped, but the echo of voices continued. You could distinguish among them the voice of the village chief, Sheikh Abdul Slam, the Quaran Reciter Mansour, and Sheikh Abdul Rahman. The masses halted surrounding Sheikh Abdul Salam, who was mounting his donkey in order to be heard.

'Listen, the Italians are behind you and in front of you. We must all say that we have seen nothing, and have heard nothing.'

From among the surrounding masses there emerged an unveiled woman carrying her baby. She managed to come nearer to Sheikh Abdul Salam.

'Sheikh, Al-Mabrouk has not come, Al-Mabrouk might be dead.'

Sheikh Abdul Salam put his hand on her shoulder to allay her fear.

'Don't be afraid. He ran away from the Italians.'

Sheikh Mansour hastily covered her head with part of his robe. Sheikh Abdul Rahman stamped his foot in frustration. A voice came from among the masses:

'I saw Al-Mabrouk tying up the captain and dragging him behind.'

The people of the village were certain that Al-Mabrouk was the hero of the day. The past few nights assured them of that. While people spent their night drinking tea, Al-Mabrouk was away. He appeared only in the very late hours, and always had someone with him, a sergeant, a soldier, or some trophy from the Italians. He often escaped death miraculously. Sheikh Abdul Salam warned him several times of the danger of these activities. He usually smiled saying:

'Don't worry, let them go down one by one.'

This very morning the Italians had found the captain of the occupying troops of the village missing. Al-Mabrouk was among those arrested after being pointed out by Robin. Robin was spying for the Italians. His eyes had been following Al-Mabrouk for days. What puzzled the population of the village was how Al-Mabrouk managed to disappear and join the fighters. His wife Salima did not know that he had escaped when she joined the villagers running away upon hearing of the Italian attack. Only now she was somewhat comforted after hearing what Sheikh Abdul Salam had to say. The dusty wind was hitting people's faces, in angry, loud gusts. The people who crowded to come closer to Abdul Salam added to the noise as they enquired about the dire situation, the killing and looting done by the Italians to the village. They were searching for their relatives. From behind the windy dust a group of Italians came nearer and surrounded them. The villagers retreated before the rumbling bullets. They fell to the ground. The children and women were frozen in fright and remained motionless. The soldiers approached Sheikh Abdul Salam upon a signal from Robin. They caught him. They spoke, addressing Sheikh Abdul Salam,

'Do you know who has killed the captain?' 'Do you know Al-Mabrouk?' The Sheikh replied, trembling,

'No. I don't know.'

The Jew translated his words to the Italian in a language Abdul Salam could not understand. The Sheikh was beaten to the ground. The Jew knelt; he whispered softly:

'Talk ... they will give you money.'

There came no answer, because Abdul Salam was unconscious. He was abandoned by the Italians who went searching in the village. Amid the wailing of women and the cries of children a number of men carried Abdul Salam and put him on his donkey. The sunset folded the village in its wings, surrounding it with darkness, silence and gloom only interrupted by bullets, cries of sorrow and fear, and the wind in the trees turned by the night into shadows. Hunger and exhaustion started to take their toll of this great march of the villagers. Children were becoming less tolerant and their cries were heard louder, causing anguish in the mothers' hearts. The old succumbed to weariness and sank down to rest. Hands held out anything available to the crying mouths of the children. Men lit some gas lamps while the wind howled, engulfing the moans of those who had been hit by bullets. A human figure was rushing through carrying something unidentifiable in the darkness. He had seen the light of the lamps from afar and made his way towards it. He came closer to the crowed of exhausted villagers. They were at first frightened to see this shadow coming from the night. Many of them overcame their weakness and stood looking at him. They soon recognised his face and shouted in one voice,

'Al-Mabrouk'

The gazing people looked in bewilderment at what he was carrying on his shoulders. A voice cried following him,

'Has he an Italian with him?'

'Tonight he has brought us a general.'

Mabrouk reached the lamplight where Sheikh Abdul Salam and a number of men stood asking,

'Is that you, Mabrouk?'

Mabrouk stood in front of them, out of breath:

'Yes, it's me, and I've brought your friend, Robin!'

They were too shocked to speak; Robin, the Italian's agent! Necks stretched to stare carefully. They soon shouted,

'It *is* Robin'.

Nobody asked how he could have caught him. They always had a feeling that Mabrouk was stronger than the Italians, stronger than their officers and their armies. Their surprise was interrupted by the voice of a woman carrying her newly born in her arms:

'Mabrouk! Mabrouk!'

Al-Mabrouk turned towards her saying,

'I am coming, Salima, I am coming.'

The darkness turned him into a moving shadow before the eyes that followed his steps. He hurried to her, took the baby in his arms, and soon disappeared completely. Behind him he left the murmuring of the tired crowd as they began to talk about Al-Mabrouk.

5

Dignity
Khalifa Takbali

The wide desert was kneeling under the drapes of the night, submitting in humiliation and silence to its might. Meanwhile the drilling rig, which was not too far from me, continued drilling enthusiastically. In vengeance and anger the drilling machine was piercing the desert and degrading it more by the removal of the living earth from its bowels.

I was sitting in the open, in front of the store watching the whispering stars, thinking, captivated by the beauty of the night that dominated my heart and mind and made me feel relaxed and happy. I was affected by the warm soft breeze which touched my face. The breeze that carried in its folds thousands of vague and anonymous letters.

I was a newcomer whether to this camp or to the other. I had never seen a desert before and so I was passionately interested in everything about it. I examined things and looked into them avidly and with a sensual delight. During the whole of my first week there I was bewitched by my new surroundings, with the people, the machines and rocks …The people, as far as I was concerned, were strangers, I neither knew nor understood them. I admired them because they were from this area and because all that dazzled me in the desert seemed to be embodied in them; it is in their blood and their naked and frank spirit. Their dark burnt faces were like the sand and their strange dry bodies were like the desert which is empty of any sign of luxury and softness.

As I was watching the night three figures appeared. They were coming, most certainly, from the direction of the noisy drilling machine … I recognised them when they entered the circle of light that shone from the store, that was behind me. The light covered me then spread over the wavy sands to a reasonable distance … They were coming towards me. I had started to watch them when they invaded my thoughts and interrupted my enjoyable wondrous imaginings. They came close to me and they surrounded me with impudence. They were three of the Americans who were working with the drilling machines. Their bodies were burnt like the sand and their clothes were shabby. They looked like tramps.

One of them asked sardonically:

'Do you have water-melon? We are in need of a water-melon.'

I knew their language and understood what they wanted. I let it appear that I did not understand. I imagined that they were begging. I asked:

'What?'

'I said water-melon. We want water-melon,' he repeated angrily.

My heart was filled with distress and I do not know why I felt cheated and restricted. Was it because of their appearance and impudence, or because of the feeling of being humiliated and compelled to carry out their desires?

What was in the store was none of my concern. I had specific instructions to provide them with everything they wanted, indeed I was bound to comply, but what hurt me most was the word 'want', that made me feel insulted and aware that I was not in my own country and that they dictated their wishes. They dictated to me in an open and insulting way. Trying to gain some time, I said:

'And what do you want with the water-melon?'

It might have been a stupid question, but their answer was indeed more stupid:

'We said that we wanted water-melon, so give it to us, and shut up.'

I had not yet decided anything. I was only trying to gain time to regain control over myself and to give them what they wanted. But despite my knowledge that I was totally rash and illogical I just couldn't help myself.

'I have no water-melon for you ... I shall give you no water-melon.'

It was not my place to say that, I knew that for sure. I knew that I was going to be punished and might even by sacked from my job because of what I had said. I was sure that in some way they would, in spite of me, take what they wanted. No matter how much I tried I would not be able to prevent them, even by force, which was in any case outside my capabilities. I knew that, but I stubbornly refused. Sometimes we behave illogically. Such behaviour is dictated by our emotions, and our minds fail to come to the rescue, despite the abundant evidence and proof of our incorrect and unproductive behaviour. Our behaviour at such times is never sensible or logical, our behaviour is childish ... just like a child who becomes angry and refuses to eat or go to school, well aware that he would be forced to do both and that it would be better for him to do so before being forced or punished.

My refusal surprised and infuriated them. They said in one
breath:
'What? ... you won't give us water-melon? ...Get up and give us
water-melon.'
I was not surprised by their amazement because I astonished
myself by my behaviour, and if I was asked to give an explanation I
would be unable. But within myself there was something that
prevented me. My heart, feelings and dignity were wounded. They
were free to take whatever they wanted, and whatever they took was
always of the choicest, and from that we, the Arabs, took the
worthless leftovers. My refusal was not for the love of water-melon
or for the fear that they might finish it, because water-melon was
abundant; but its abundance was for us, the Arabs. The foreigners
did not eat it. They ate different kinds of fruits, better and tastier.
Every day they ate different kinds of fruits, whereas we used to eat
water-melon with two meals a day. All that they took was the
choicest and according to their wants; as for us we could not ask for
more than our share. Sometimes I wished that I could have what
they ate. I felt resentful and envious of them, but I always repressed
my feelings. I told myself that they were technicians and that their
salaries were high, therefore they had the right to eat better ... so
why then water-melon?'
I felt that they wanted to insult me on purpose. Why the water-
melon? They do not eat it. They cannot enjoy it beside the other
fruits given to them ... Why then? They had taken their share. I gave
them sufficient amounts at supper. Why then did they want more?
And why water-melon in particular?
I said:
'No ... I will not give you water-melon ... Go away, you have
eaten ... and I am not going to give you any more.'
One of them ironically approached me ready to strike. His body
was strong and muscular. He was always half naked because either
he loved his body or the tattoos that covered it. Struck by fear I drew
back a short distance. My situation was hopeless. They were three
and I was alone ... Even if I were to beat them they would arrest me
and accuse me of being provocative if any riots were to take place.
'Be careful. Don't hit me. I have no water-melon. Go to the
manager – I do not have any water-melon.'
He did not stop his slow advance. I, too, did not stop my
withdrawal. I was frightened and ready. If he was going to hit me I
would hit him back ... I was thinking of what I should do. How was
I going to evade his punch?

'You are going to give us water-melon ...huh ... say that you are going to give us water-melon.'

I said, while looking behind me for fear that I might trip and fall:

'Don't be stupid ... I am not going to give you water-melon ... I do not have any.'

'We will see ... You will find the water-melon and give it to us ... We want it.'

In my retreat I reached the wall of the store. I could go no further backwards. Unconsciously I reclined on the iron wall as if to relax.

Fear tired me and my nerves were shattered and strained. My heart was beating fast. I was thinking of what I must do. It was not easy to back down now. I wished that I was able to say:

'Let me see ... There might be some water-melon.'

But I was not able. I was too proud to let him see my humiliation. I imagined that he would laugh at me. He would make fun of me and would say:

'Bring it then.'

He came very close to me. He stood with clenched fists threatening me:

'Give me the water-melon. I am telling you. The best thing ... give me the water-melon. Give me the key. I shall take the water-melon.'

He was angry in an abominable way. His red puffed and insulted face was very close to me. His eyes glinted with authority and mastery. My fright grew. I felt the weight of his anger and the possible outcome. I had a vague feeling which grew from their carefree behaviour and haughtiness, that it was possible for him to commit a foolish act. He might even kill me. I did not have the power to humiliate my ego. I said:

'No. I will not give you the key. It is not your right to take the key.'

'Very well. I ...'

He moved his naked muscular arm with the speed of lightning. I dodged the punch which hit my shoulder painfully and went on to hit the iron wall. That made him explode with anger.

'You are the most contemptible Arab pig I have ever seen ... I will show you.'

His words fell upon me and pricked me ... He had touched something that was hidden. I was blinded with anger.

'You contemptible American ... you ...'

I got nearer to him – I did not know how – I had lost my senses. I could not see anything any more. He withdrew. He was frightened of me. I was possessed by an evil pride, and I advanced, brandishing my arm in readiness to squash him.

The other two came to his side. They said with mockery:

'Kill him. He wants to play, so we will play with him.'

They felt safe because they were three and I was alone. Raising their fists in the air with their lips parted they confidently came towards me in a challenging and mocking way. I felt the danger and withdrew a step while they were advancing. I looked around me as if I were calling for help, calling the sand of my country and urging it to rise to my help. But the sand appeared as if it were helping them. The sand was hindering my steps and made me trip in its uneasy waves.

I saw a heavy rod of metal thrown carelessly, calling me. Without giving a thought to anything else I moved quickly to pick it up. I held it in my hand and advanced towards them, mad with anger.

'Now come nearer, you despicable ... Come nearer so I can crush your skulls, you vile Americans ...Come on ...'

My anger was raging. All that I had suffered throughout my life, the xenophobia, the inferiority complex, exploded in a moment of unconsciousness, wounded pride, and suppressed hatred.

The rod of iron gave me a feeling of superiority so I no longer feared them. Yet they kept coming on towards me with some caution and without fear.

Unconsciously I drew back, an instinctive cowardice came over me but I very soon came to and took control of myself. I was provoked by their advance. I felt their contempt of me, their contempt of all of us. I felt something burning in my heart.

With madness I hit the one who was nearest to me with hatred and malice. The heavy iron rod fell on his shoulder. He fell to the ground weak and broken.

I shouted, and inside me there was an illogical and roaring happiness for victory.

'Cowards ... you are in my country ... I will show you that you are in my country.'

They withdrew a few steps back leaving their colleague behind. This made me drunk with power. I had defeated them. I felt that it was possible for me to be victorious over them. I, then, went off following them, shouting with a frenzied desire for killing and bloodshed.

The noise attracted attention, so they all came from their tents to watch the fight. The manager and the chief of the camp came and asked me the reason for the quarrel. I said, with the innocence of a child: 'They wanted our water-melon, and I would not give them the water-melon.'

6

'Come, Let Me Whisper in Your Ear'
Sayed Gaddaf-Addam

Come let us cast aside radio sets, news of the world, newspapers and peace talks, the trivialities of aspirers and the sanctimony of fools; leave aside the prying of the inquisitive, bugging devices, and the ignorant – leave all this and that, let us discuss matters together without a chairman or opinion-transmitting devices or loudspeakers. Let us move all these contrivances and talk.

My princess, allow me to speak and do not interrupt me. Let me go on and do not let me get accustomed to your being a chatterer, unable to stem the flow of words when they gush forth; for I no longer care what happens to a 'hundred and one things', just as I no longer care what occurs a few metres away from me. I do not heed what ministers proclaim, or plans for development, or politics, or those with conflicting orders; for I am, my lady, a tired compatriot, exhausted with all the things that control us and make us lose the ability even to express an opinion, and transform us into parrots repeating what is said without understanding.

These things, my friend, are what control us now and deprive us of the enjoyment of things: the sweetness of life, the taste of contentment; the frame which encloses us has now become our master, forcibly causing us to commit errors under the guise of good intentions and experience.

Let us cast aside these things, come and listen for the first time to the roar of the sea, the chanting of angels, and let us see moonlight for the first time, and listen to our folk songs as they issue forth from the mouths of shepherds, not the mouths of the rabble. Let us take handfuls of sand in our hands to scatter in any direction. Let us see with our own eyes nature, stones and wild grasses.

Let us cancel today's and all future appointments without prior notice and change our abodes, and forget all our present friends for they are merely acquaintances serving their own benefit.

Let us start from zero, and disappear from the world for a few hours, then return to see it afresh. Let me call you by a new name which no one has ever used before, and let me give you an age of my own making; for I do not know our present ages, nor do I acknowledge them, because the mere acknowledgement of them is to be lost and to slide to the bottom of an abyss. Our present ages mean nothing except desolate years we have lived from our actual childhood to our contained childhood.

My friend, let us leave the bright lights aside and search for a deserted place. Let us inhale air from its original sources instead of breathing it through windows and air conditioners. Let us live the simple life of the Bedouin and leave complicated equipment, and the complexities of the city. Let us talk and address each other with our own tongues, not the tongues of others, and write with our own pens, not the pens of others.

Let us record our knowledge with charcoal on cardboard, and roam in every direction; and let our hands clasp firmly in agreement over things. Come ... let me dress you in a pink robe for a winter siesta.

My princess, allow me to smell perfume through the folds of your clothes, and let me tease you with obscure words which defy simple interpretation. I once asked about Woman, and found her the other side of Man; but the women I had seen in my city were but a collection of hollow pieces of wood covered with articles of adornment.

Cast aside women, adornments, pieces of wood, and all the aforementioned. Let us place our fingers over our lips and withdraw quietly from everybody. There is no prayer except in a chancel, and no doors ever open for strangers but in a mosque; just as there is no true happiness in the cementitious environment of the twentieth century.

Come let us draw up particular specifications for the children of the future. Let us draw the colour of their eyes, and hair, and choose beautiful names for them.

Let us stand out in the open and allow the wind to ruffle my necktie and your hair; for I am suffocating in this air of interwoven events and its features which alter from one instant to the next.

Let us run far away until, tired and exhausted, we fall upon the ground, not on easy chairs or anything that elevates us above the earth, for we are from it and we shall return to it, even should we die in lofty constructions.

My little princess, things are not as you see them, or as passers-by see them; and the happy are those with power and wealth. They are the unhappy ones, especially the undeserving of them. Happiness is not something that comes to us from the outside. It springs from within our being. You see happiness in the smile of a child. You see it in the shyness of a girl on her first meeting with her beloved. You see it in the eyes of the innocent when they face the one who rules them.

Allow me to see God in your eyes once more, my lady; do not raise your voice too much while speaking, for the voices of others are most annoying because they are so loud. Try to withstand, in spite of your limitations, the length of the journey. Let us sail in a primitive boat on the ocean. Let us discard our complications and problems, our fear of ignorance and of the unknown, come let us make sure that we follow the right path, and dream of our own paradise. Let us construe things at their truth and originate all things to God, for He is their maker, and our creator. Man cannot, no matter what power he attains, define the value of happiness permitted us, or the degree of evil with which God tests us. No doubt we shall mock them, those human beings who commit evil and lead their lives in malice. Let us pity them at the same time for God has chosen them as spiteful instruments of evil with mastery over mankind.

My lady, you are a beauty who suddenly materialised in a desert called Libya, and a natural moon which suddenly appeared in a pitch-black night, and a magnificent poem delivered in 'Uqadh (the ancient poetry gathering). You are the most beautiful decision to start a relationship among women.

You are all the women I have known in their goodness and their evil, in their beauty and their ugliness, in their purity and their corruption, in their virtue and their wickedness; you are my own self in spite of the differences of class which separate us, for there is no difference between us, regardless of the conflicting language which claims that class differences exist, and breach of promises.

You asked me to define Woman? She is the most beautiful contradiction that God created, so forsake anxiety, and free yourself from the constrictions of doubt. Meet me in the usual place under the moonlight.

Wear whatever you wish when we meet, and I shall put on what I want. We won't be restricted by the dictates of fashion. Arrive by any means possible. Let us roam the city like two runaway children searching for a safe place to hide.

Come, let us sit like two strangers in public places, and laugh for all people, and only cry for the poor and the wronged.

Come let us exchange topics of conversation without an observer or eye witness. Come let us establish human relationships as God intended them to be and reject the advice of the ridiculous 'Sheikh', the dowry and wedding festivities. Let us practice happiness as we imagine it and visualise it. Let us eat what we like, let us cancel night and hours and start afresh. Let us unite our living desires, which do not conflict with the desires of other human beings. Let us take off our old shoes and walk barefoot, digging our feet until they sink into the sand.

Come let us do something out of the ordinary, let us switch off the radio and the TV, and tear up newspapers and despise those who overpower, the inquisitive, and those who occupy themselves with trivialities, and let us walk in the desert.

My friend, let us cancel our past allegiances to all things, except to a merciful God. Let us attend the Friday speech together and make fun of the ridiculous speaker who promises us of 'houris', and makes us anxious to meet them, for these thoughts are merely physical.

Come let us be certain that we are alive, for I have some doubt that we are.

Let us destroy our personal records, travel visas, and identity papers and let us cancel all information originating from others about us and view people afresh as it pleases us.

Come let us taste sea water, perhaps it is not as salty as we have been told. Let us submerge ourselves in the depth of the sea where our people fear to enter; let us make mistakes as we please and let others punish us as they please, under the pretext of the law. Let us contravene traffic signals, and flout conventions which separate men from women.

Let us name things as we want and as we please, and let us acquaint ourselves with what people know.

Let us look again at things.

At war and peace.

At summit meetings and at disarmament.

At regression and progression; the adventurous left, the crooked right; and the collapsing middle. Let us place all these things into one pot, mix them, and serve them afresh as a new kind of food at the table of the United Nations.

Let us search the shops of the city, and throw away all artificial flowers, and use a new currency with the sales people. Let us unite for ourselves and in spite of ourselves.

Let us live to discern the truth not as we read in Colin Wilson's books. And let us live 'Nausea' as we feel it, not as Sartre felt it. And let us really suffer and not as we were told by Frantz Fanon.

Let us take a stand in this life which was forced upon us. Let us break the yoke, and cancel lunch and supper and breakfast, and make the former the latter and what is contrary true.

Let us compete at poetry, not at politics and dispose of the dead words of the language which writers have destroyed and laughed at.

Let us invent new terms for parting and meeting, for greetings and good manners.

Let us sit alone like two opposite poles which do not meet except once.

Let us deviate from the norm and tolerate what others say about us and feel happiness at opposing what is trivial.

My friend, who is sad to her depths, smiling only on the surface: God does not want misery for us, but we create if for ourselves. God brought us down to this world, and preferred us to all creatures, but we reject this preference and go to war, and the betrayal of principles, and tittle-tattle. God, my little one, invites us to all the events for doing good, but we refuse the invitation and punctually attend the invitations of the devil.

The compatriots in my city gather in Mecca to stone the devil within a circle, forgetting they stone themselves in every direction.

I need, my lady, time to convince sinners that they are the opposite of what they expect. Help me to stand and don't leave me alone for loneliness is deadly.

Do not let me suffer from you too much; suffice it what I suffer from other men and the pen.

Let me touch your hair and play with it and run my fingers through it, then braid it into two long pigtails like two sad ribbons in the desert of emotions.

Teach me how to read and how to write, even how to hold a pen. Teach me the complete alphabet and the incomplete, and with letters unlike those which I learnt from the scribe at the mosque. Teach me how to think aloud and how to use my thoughts to our advantage; and push away evil spirits with your sweet hands. Help me to understand the world. Let us discuss it and arrive at suggested solutions then choose the ideal one and follow it.

Repeat what I have told you to make sure that you are with me. Mix up my words and let them mingle, then sort them out and arrange them as you please.

See me pray for you.

And worship at your chancel, pour out my words then go to sleep, enclosing my image within your eyelids. My words grow pure in your hands. Address me with your conscience, not his conscience, or hers.

Preserve our things within both hands. Let me dream, and rave, and write.

I ask you from my depths to comprehend life anew. I call you to celebrate the feast and every happy occasion on which I invite you to prepare for adventure. For life without adventure is worthless. Come let us take with us our modest possessions and aim for an unknown destination.

I ask your permission to study the woman in you, learning your features. Let me observe the opposite sex as I see it, not as others say it is. Let my hands feel everything in you and make certain that nature has not deserted you as the papers and beauty advertisements claim. Let us tolerate this life together, and don't let the weight of responsibility fall entirely upon the man as happens here.

Let us ascend to the minaret of the mosque and look down upon the people below from our height and drive in carriages pulled by horses led by an old man who never looks back.

I entrust you to carry these words to the children of the future because our present adolescents have already been moulded and conditioned. It is difficult to undo the damage.

Life starts for us with the joyous cries of celebration at birth, and ends with wailing and weeping at death, with a grand void between them.

7

The Road
Yousif Al Sharif

'MAKE ROOM! Clear the road, you who don't know its hardships!'

He utters these words as if he were the only one who suffered from the road's cruelty. He tries to move a step forward, but the bodies that jostle around him in other directions hinder him. He turns round to assure himself that all is well, that no devilish hand is going to snatch one or more of the Italian apples from the boxes – he imagines this could happen, despite the fact that they are in sealed boxes. Should this happen, he would have to make good the loss. He has to deliver the boxes safely and soundly to their final destination. Afterwards he will receive no more than ten piastres. 'From the Tuesday market to "Fashloom" – all this for ten piastres!'

He shakes his head in disbelief … 'Make room! Clear the road, you who don't know its hardships!'

The cart sways to the right and to the left and his heart beats fast … Oh Protector … he spits on the ground as he secretly curses the progeny of the impetuous youth who was pushed by one of his friends and chose to fall over the cart. Had he not maintained its balance at the last minute, a disaster would have happened. He feels the thick rope pressing painfully on his shoulder.

He had hoped for a whole year to buy a beast of burden to pull the cart instead of hauling it himself but that wish vanished. He tried more than once throughout last year to save ten piastres a day, but having returned several times without money in his pocket, he had to abandon the idea. 'Make room! Clear the road! You who don't know its hardships!'

His foot stumbles on a stone and the pain nearly brings tears to his eyes. He rubs the injured foot with the other one to ease the pain and with a sudden, violent, rebellious movement, jerks the cart forward. Once again he thinks of the crowds with their slowness that arouses his resentment and sense of futility. Several thoughts race through his head to gain control: how long will he remain in charge of this disgraceful cart, which costs him two piastres a day to hire? He frees his right hand and feels his shoulder … those tormentors who refuse to make way for him! If only one of them had to pull the

47

cart just once, they would soon experience the degree of his suffering! He whose fate it was to pull it several times each day. He halts when he reaches a bend in the road and pulls, but the cart refuses to move, as if it was nailed to the ground. He tries again but the cart will not budge. He takes the rope off his shoulder and goes to the back to investigate. He finds that four children had been clinging on to it but they out-race the wind the instant they see him rushing towards them. He replaces the rope round his shoulder as storms of rage howl in his depths and the image of his children, Ali and Muhammad, floats in his mind; their long wait for him each day and their sneaking a secret ride on the cart ... not only that, but when things didn't go well for him, especially on Tuesdays and Fridays, he would fill the cart with children from the street on his way back home.

He feels that tears would betray him should he continue to think about such things. He had never wept in his life, not even as a child when he was assaulted by a British soldier. He did not cry but picked up a large, solid stone and nearly brained him with it.

Once when a traffic patrolman wrote out a fine because he drove the cart through Martyrs Square, he still did not cry or beg for mercy. 'Make room! Clear the road, you who don't know its hardships!'

What has happened to people? Why do they persist in obstructing him? He stops for a while to assure himself that the apples are safe and counts the boxes for maybe the hundredth time, then he advances slowly, people's loud voices and shouts increasing the tautness of his nerves and his pain. If only he could get out of this hell! He exerts a greater effort and attempts to increase his speed, but the cart shakes and judders so violently, his heart nearly stops beating. He must save his load more than his own life. Should any damage befall it – God forbid – he would have to spend days and nights in jail as a punishment. The owner of the apples had threatened him so, and he was in no doubt that he would carry out his promise should anything ... ouch! He stubs his foot on another accursed stone ... he must concentrate his attention solely on the load in the cart, if he knew what was good for him. 'Make room! Clear the road, you who don't know its hardships!'

He repeats these words in a voice charged with entreaty and pain several times a day ... but despite this everybody refuses to make way for him. He looks to the left and to the right and advances, his fears over the load increasing with each step he takes. Thoughts and imaginings never giving him an opportunity to relax. A deadly anxiety possesses him. His thoughts take him far ... far away, cause him to forget his precious load. Yet the path of his life, a large part of which had been spent pulling his cart, and another large part moving between the British army camps and the local ones, this he cannot forget. He also cannot forget the long days spent looking for work to no avail. All these things make him think and think until he is exhausted.

He remembered the first day he went to the Haj* asking him to rent the cart, and the Haj's insistence that he pay a deposit of three piastres – his retreat to the quarter where he lived, his gathering the remnants of his clothes and those of his wife plus her silver dowry – the only things she had left since her marriage. Then his going to the market and the hours spent haggling over them in a voice overladen with curses and defiance, the eyes of those who knew him smarting him with their cruel reproach. He was certain the news would spread like wildfire in the neighbourhood, but that did not bother him then. He sold the clothes and the jewellery for two piastres, and returned home, in utter despair and it was only with the entreaties of some friends that the Haj grudgingly accepted the two piastres.

'Make room! Clear the road, you who don't know its hardships!' The strong aroma of the Italian apples assails him. He remembers that he has never tasted an apple in his life! What would happen if he took just one? He nearly carries out his intent but when he sees the boxes defying him with their sealed flimsy wooden covers, he retreats ... his yearning and longing for one increasing. He whips round in a lingering movement, his eyes searching the faces of passers-by, as if saying to them: 'Does my suffering please you?' 'Make room! Clear the road, you who don't know its hardships!'

He feels an overwhelming happiness as he discovers himself occupying the middle of the road, car hooters following him persistently to let them pass. He deliberately slows his pace, smiling with satisfaction, but when he sees a policeman moving towards him his smile vanishes and he quickens his step. Hopes, which so often toyed with his imagination, now invade his thoughts, turning to bitter anguish, arousing in his very being the eternal question: 'Why are our wishes never fulfilled?' Why? Even though they are modest and trivial? ... Is he to remain in charge of this cart always? Pulling it from sunrise to sunset till the last day of his life? Why? Did he do something to deserve all this punishment? ... He was a good person

---

* 'Haj' is a title given to a person who has made the Holy Pilgrimage to Mecca. He is usually a man of standing and prestige in the community, well-off financially to be able to afford the trip.

... liking people and wishing them happiness ... and suffering for them. 'Still, never mind, trust time. The path of everything changes.'

He stops for a while watching each side of the road then plunges on. Just before he turns a corner, he feels something solid smash against his forehead. He staggers backwards and feels a sharp pain in his foot. The cart shakes violently and tilts, overturning some boxes, but he pushes his arms against it until it straightens then he proceeds to put the boxes back on. He wishes he could chase the rascal who seizes this opportunity to snatch an apple, or does he? During all this some passers-by have begun to converge and crowd around him. He feels parts of his body start to disjoint from each other. He puts a hand to his forehead and it turns red, the pain increasing and his legs begin to give way. The looks in the eyes that surround him remind him of those of the Haj, the owner of the cart. He tears a long strip of cloth off his robe and carefully bandages his head. To the amazement of the eyes that watch him and in spite of the intensity of the pain, he bends forward and pulls the cart. Before any of the passers-by utter a sound, he shouts at them: 'Make room! Clear the road, you who don't know its hardships!' and disappears down the long road!

8

She and the Dogs
Ibrahim el Kouni

Eve ... our ancient mother, come to my help.
What beautiful legs made of marble.
How lovely your body of crystal.

In the beginning she didn't pay any attention to him. Then she turned out of curiosity. He was as emaciated as a hungry wolf, his teeth bared; he was thin and medium-built; he was like a mangy dog in the dark.

She had been waiting for an hour, the long hand of her watch was creeping toward 10, it still wasn't 10 o'clock. She remembered the struggle that was still going on between the Nasr Company and the local newspapers. She thought that the press had really exaggerated in their depiction of the company's ineptitude – but now – after being subjected to the tardiness of the small bus – she realised the truth of their criticism. And furthermore, here she was having to bear the common flirtations of street wolves prowling through the night.

Cars raced past her, the drivers of them blinking their lights, braking, then stinging her with their glances – their eyes gleaming like flame, stabbing at her like needles, prickling her skin, seeking her nakedness – while for the sake of Eve ... he tried again with mad persistence.

'No use waiting ... the bus won't come, three buses are out of order, and the rest stop running after nine o'clock. I've been standing at the August 9th Square station for so long now.'

She didn't turn, didn't utter a sound, didn't act concerned. She built a solid wall of silence.

'I have a friend who lives nearby. We'll go there and he'll give you a lift – he's got a car.'

Idiot. Dope. Stupid. She had heard these reprisals a thousand times, she had repeated them scornfully along with her friends – most likely it must have been a million times. Anecdotes were made of them in the caricatures found on the last page of the newspaper. She glanced on the last page of the newspaper. She glanced at her wristwatch ... 10 o'clock. Cats were crossing the street, climbing the garbage cans, prowling around them, urinating on the pavement. The green and red of the traffic lights stopped their alternate exchange and were replaced with the yellow, flicking on and off in the darkness, as if somebody were winking at her. The night was calm and still except for the occasional barking of dogs straying amidst the alleys of the old city.

Waiting was useless. She turned and started to cross Omar al-Mukhtar Street. She strained her ears. The stranger didn't follow her.

Just before Bank di Roma she heard their whispers, the beginning of a whisper, suggesting the plotting of a conspiracy. Their feet moved in the same direction, then quickened in pace, then they began running. They bolted toward her like some legendary animal who had gone hungry for a million years and was now stalking a prey who had suddenly fallen down from the sky. They surged forward, came nearer and nearer. She turned in high-pitched horror, but she only saw pitch-black darkness. She set off running ... running ... she gasped for air ... she ran until her legs became numb ... as solid as rocks. Her handbag flipped open, her cosmetics tumbled to the ground as well as her money purse and a report (called 'Steps toward the liberation of the Libyan woman') which she had prepared for a sociology lecture – everything fell out until her handbag was empty. But she just kept on running and didn't stop until she found herself in the perfumeries shop.

She flung herself violently over the wooden bench, gasping for breath, her heart contracting as if she had just travelled some incredible distance in the blink of an eye, as quickly as Suleiman's magic genie. She opened her eyes and saw him standing over her, staring at her with a mixture of surprise and artificial compassion, while she realised what had happened. He didn't speak immediately, he understood her predicament and brought her a glass of water. She saw the prayer beads in his hand, and thanked God that there were still some decent people around, that there were still decent folk on this earth. She mumbled something incomprehensible, even to herself. She took the glass of water and took a sip; then she sighed a couple of times and said,

'I am sorry, sir, they were chasing me.'

He stood staring at her stupidly without saying a word, while anger grew inside her at the dullness of his reaction. She repeated, as if she were making a plea to be rescued from legendary beasts:

'They were chasing me, really they were, and I'm afraid.'

He twirled his prayer beads in the air and spoke for the first time:

'Who was chasing you?'

'I don't know who, but they were hiding behind the store in the dark, waiting to ambush me ... help me!'

He went towards the door and looked to right and left and returned while she was standing up:

'Well ... I didn't see anyone.'

'But I heard them from here whispering to one another.'

'You must be tired. Sit down, my child ... You're imagining things.'

She was overcome by violent anger:

'I'm not imagining things. They chased me to the door and hid themselves behind the store next door.'

She moved towards the door. He followed, she paused and pointed to the darkness.

'They were whispering to one another, conspiring in the night!'

'My dear, I didn't see anything at all. You were seeing illusions. Sit down ... rest a bit.'

She screamed:

'You're blind, I wasn't hallucinating. They chased after me up to here. They were guarding the wall waiting for me. I saw them with my own eyes.'

Astonishment and anger flared in his eyes. She collapsed over the chair and began to shiver. Soon tears started to stream down her face, and she apologised meekly:

'I'm very sorry, I didn't mean ...'

'It doesn't matter, don't worry. Rest a while. Don't be afraid, I'm right here beside you ... would you like some coffee or tea?'

'No, thank you.'

Silence reigned for a few moments before he enquired in a meaningful tone:

'Was it really necessary for you to go out by yourself at this time of night?'

'It wasn't late. The bus was late. I left my aunt's house at 9 o'clock.'

He fingered his beads. Through his to-so-dark glasses he stole glances which scrutinised every inch of her body from top to bottom ... for the first time she noticed that he wore glasses, he must be blind ... he brought forward a wooden chair and sat opposite her. Until that moment she hadn't felt secure or sensitive toward him, had hoped that she would be able to treat him as a father figure.

'You can stay here until morning ...there's a room inside.' He cleared his throat while noticing the doubt and disapproval in her eyes. He decided to dispel them by saying in his kindest and most innocent tone:

'I'll sleep here in the store on a mat.'
She trembled, resisting like a bird in a cage.
'No, no … I really must go, my husband's expecting me.'
He said, while his eyes fell despairingly on the wedding finger:
'As you like … whatever is best for you.'
He continued to encircle her in his glances, in loathsome lingering looks … for the sake of Eve, as if he were waiting for her to excuse herself and go away as long as she refuses his proposition. He was throwing her out … threatening her with his glances; she must face the dogs who are waiting behind the wall to ambush her. She said to him, pleading:
'Please call the police for me. I'm afraid to go out alone.'
He continued to besiege her – to consume her. The bird that fell from the sky was just about to fly from the cage, to escape forever. He said after hesitating:
'All right.'
He began dialling.
The car braked and a police officer with the rank of second sergeant stepped out … he went toward the store's entrance. He stood on the threshold. The hard-line features of his face softened and bore the beginning traces of an amiable smile. He entered, grabbed a chair and sat down without a word of protocol, as if it were his shop and he could act as he pleased. He took a pack of cigarettes out of his pocket, offering one to her a gesture preceded by the ready-made smile which became immediately a choked laugh. She was quick to deny the accusation of a cigarette, as if she were denying herself (or another self) implicated in the action of smoking. As if she were fleeing from spider webs which were beginning to strangle her.
'No …no, thank you. I can't stand cigarettes.'
He withdrew his smile as he drew back the offered pack of cigarettes. He pulled out a cigarette for himself, ignoring the shop-owner completely. He puffed out the smoke in little rings and looked at her before asking:
'Where do you live?'
'In Green Hill."
'OK. Let's go.'
He rose, trying to cover his face in a veil of seriousness and decisiveness, but the air of complicity was obvious in his eyes, or so it seemed to her. She was suffocated now by an insurmountable terror of accompanying him; she was quick to discover that her body moved inside a snake skin or frog skin, it was sticky and she felt like

vomiting.

'No ... please call me a taxi, that's a better idea.'

The policeman exchanged looks with the shop-owner. The shop-owner shrugged his shoulders in denial of the accusation.

'She is the one who wanted me to call the police. Ask her.'

The officer shifted his eyes from one to the other, a dark anger storming his brow, and then said in a commanding tone:

'Request a taxi for her.'

A sleek car braked to a stop in front of the store. A heavy-set man got out. He was stout and had thick lips. The mere sight of him could only induce feelings of repulsion. She left the store and stepped quickly inside the taxi without saying a word to the shop-owner. The officer instructed the taxi-driver:

'Take her to Green Hill.'

Then he winked.

She

After spending a two-month honeymoon in Paris, Ahmed said to her in a gently mocking tone:

'How long are you going to continue challenging traditional customs by chasing behind the latest fashions and mixing with men, staying out late with your girlfriends and others as the European women do?'

She answered defiantly:

'What is the difference between a European woman and me, at least intellectually speaking, if we have both read Kafka, Neruda, Nietzsche, Hemingway, and Sartre? I'm a serious woman, even if I like fashion and soirées and you know that.'

'I didn't mean to demean your behaviour or your earnestness, but the societies differ. That's where the tragedy lies – that our society is not like European societies.'

Only a week before a colleague of hers, Abbas al-Misrati, told her during a heated discussion about the Libyan woman:

'I am not content with the liberation of the woman if it is not radical, for liberation in a backward feudal society like ours is only a false liberation, one which is not genuine ... your problem is that you are stubborn ... they shall make you pay the price for that!'

At Bab Ben Ghasir, the car swerved left in a wild turn and rushed ahead along a road lined by tall thickly-branched trees. She screamed out because she was so startled, and then, muffled herself as if she had submitted.

Then she gathered all her strength and shouted:

'Stop! I said slow down.'

He appeared to take notice of her severely objective tone. He said without turning round:

'I know there's another way to al-Hadhba, but it's closed. I'm taking the detour I know.'

He started speeding up again, but she said:

'Stop ... I'm getting out.'

He pushed the pedal down further.

'Stop ... I want to get out.'

The maddening velocity of the car increased.

'Stop ... Are you deaf?'

The car raced with the wind ... it flew in the air.

'Stop – you're crazy.'

She grabbed his neck.

She ran ... she ran until she could no longer breathe, but she kept on running. Even though her handbag dropped behind she kept on running.

She and He

The key was lost with her handbag ... she knocked on the door until he opened it, while still trying to open his sleepy eyes.

'Why are you late?'

'It's nothing ... the bus was late as usual.'

He returned to lie down on the bed and closed his eyes.

She

However, Laila, for the first time in her life, couldn't sleep at all that night, she couldn't enjoy the respite of a night's sleep and her eyelids didn't droop until the morning ... she just stared at the ceiling all night. She was sensitive to the fact that she had lost something for the first time ... lost something important ... a legendary wall had crumbled and fell somewhere deep within her ...

9

Signatures on Flesh
K H Mustafa

I thought I had heard that voice before, that same voice which now echoes in the air ... wavering slowly – breaking – rising violently, then dwindling – a howling and a convulsion – disintegrating into short cries.

The same voice now orders me to stand in a row with a sharp note which grates like a creaking sound – I am taken by surprise at the order and the situation as a whole, in particular the command to join a long human column which issued from no particular person nor a specific source – suffice it that it was a stern order – conveying a threatening note – oblivious of the possibility of refusal or its consequences – this was what I could not easily accept – but it did not cross my mind to do so.

I had been sauntering without a care – I remembered a rude joke and was about to laugh to myself – when I collided with the voice once more – a curse and a fury – the echo of contempt – so fierce and stunning as to strike a person dumb.

It was as if I had lost my senses or as though the situation possessed magical powers. I instantly doubled back and moved without turning round towards the human wall – and stood at the back – I was the last one. I started to wipe the cold sweat that covered my neck and forehead as the booming voice faded away and a tense silence hung overhead. Nothing moved or gave any sign of life down the length of the human chain. Nothing was heard apart from the creaking of the glass door which opened periodically to swallow one of the men – he who enters is not seen emerging again – after a while – once more – confronting perplexity, anxiety and frozen sweat.

To pass the time which hung heavily and to overcome the feelings of weariness and bewilderment, I sank into a clamorous discourse with myself.

He who now stands at the end of the line is an unknown person who has acquired a magical quality – a mere unfortunate employee – myself – a statue made of fragile clay – absorbing air and time, dozing over the headlines of daily newspapers – merging into the crowds and watching people as they scurry and sleep and breed on a

57

large bed – quarrelling with the days and stripping the skins of women – converging on the edge of the bed when time lay vacant and chattering – the bedspread gets soiled – is cleansed with rain – which the sun then dries – and no sooner does the body of a man or woman fall over the edge of the bed – than several heavily-veined hands lift the body and place it into a dark wooden box with a secure lid then discard it far away.

The men then wave their hands in boredom and once more converge in the middle of the bed to recount the sins of the person just departed – unbeknown to him – to God's mercy.

Every morning the clay statue repeats his monotonous game – he slips into a dusty suit and pats his head then emerges into the street – surprised each time at how constrained he is – that's why we see him contriving arguments with walls and vehicles – he fixes his gaze on balconies – the balconies get reflected in his eyes – and he explodes with fright when he discovers that in every balcony there is the body of a dead girl – and the clay statue which was born of mud swears that he would never again sink his eyes into dead flesh – or provoke war with stones, shadows, vehicles and stars devoid of light.

Every day the statue renews its solid oath but … there again is that accursed voice rising up, twisted and intrusive: 'Don't put your hands in your pockets!'

I obeyed the order waiting for a miracle to happen and for the fog to disperse – and that I can solve the riddle from above – to see its face and stare at its features and bathe it in light – I will return to my mother and recount the whole episode but she won't believe anything I say – for my mother had always assured me that the bed which accommodates everything, does not tolerate funny lies in the end.

The line starts to decrease – those who enter do not come out again – nobody separates me from the door except one man – it's the same frightened man – to whose heart beats I had been listening and which sound like an old clock – he was really so terrified that he trembled when I whispered in his ear, asking him about the glass door and what the large building contained – he trembled and said nothing.

Eventually he crept inside the creaking glass door – I remained alone – the sun had departed and long shadows spread over the land – a cold wind was blowing – surrounding the building with a desolate darkness.

The door opened for the last time and I entered – all sense of fear

disappeared from me – I took a few steps along a dimly lit corridor –
and all over the walls were scattered various jumbled writings.

I started to read what was written in a bad scrawl – distinguishing
words with difficult – luminous red dots separated words and
sentences.

'Attention ...'

'Laughter is an outmoded habit ...'

'Don't try to understand – attempting to understand is a
misfortune.'

'Mask – any mask.'

'Night is the mask.'

I was filled with sorrow because I understood nothing, and I
crossed the corridor pursued by despair – I slunk into a large hall
empty of all furniture – a lamp was hanging from the ceiling pouring
its light over the body of a naked woman – lying stretched out – with
legs wide open on the marble floor without moving. I approached
the woman with trepidation – I had imagined at first that what I was
seeing was a daydream – the mysterious woman – the vision of
those who die suddenly – embalmed longing, the burning
anticipation on the edge of the large bed – spilt blood – then ... then
there was the woman, unforbidden and available.

I leapt over the short distance – looking down on the exposed
illuminated nakedness – giggling in astonishment – recalling those
who had passed here before me – not remembering their number –
but this is not important now – all the waiting in the sun and the
harsh voice – all that has now ended in this long-imagined banquet
of flesh.

I shakily bent over her – and extended a trembling hand – my
pulsating blood mingling with my sweat and rapid breathing – time
stood still – my dear mother would never believe my story – I
approached the accursed woman – and my head fell between my
hands – suddenly as if plummeting from a mountain – I discovered
that the woman was dead – a naked rigid body.

All this beauty without warmth – an extinguished fire – the long
hair without a sheen – with the touch of wood – its roughness and
pallid colour.

The breasts were clustered on the chest, flaccid and shrunken –
without a sparkle or a glimmer or a shiver – spread open to silence,
death and disappointment – waiting for an invasion that would not
occur – a rain drizzle soon dried by the air – waiting for blood to
course through their veins – a closed passage.

No doubt a devil had arranged this trick – I clasped my head in my hands – and at that moment the familiar voice repeated in contrived dignity and a solemn resonance:

'Place your signature on the body and leave the room at once!'

I could not muster any strength to move my fingers ... either a signature or death.

'Time is running out.'

I resumed staring at the flesh, this mummified piece of flesh, and noticed in that instant that all those who had preceded me into this hall had left behind them their signatures and fingerprints. I noticed small circles and twisted interwoven lines and some drops of slimy saliva on the body – the carcass was covered with red blotches as if they had been caused by savage livid pinch-marks.

Some had not been content with merely pinching – but had sunk their teeth into the dead flesh.

I fled from the hall – fighting to control my sobs but a strange laugh burst behind my bent frame – a melodious soft laugh – it was the woman who a short while ago was lying with legs wide apart waiting for the rain – the deceased woman who bore the signatures of the whole population of the city all over her body – she had returned to life suddenly and was laughing seductively.

I dried my tears and turned round back towards the hall – but my way was obstructed by the booming voice which burst forth and shook the whole building down to its foundations.

'It was your only chance but you missed it and you must depart from the building instantly.'

I departed leaving nothing behind me except my disappointment and the rotting body – and the stern voice which kept on repeating incessantly:

'To live like a human you only get one chance ... To live ...'

I left that mythical building and have not been able so far to escape from the mould of clay which I had inherited from my father and my grandfather.

10

The Choice
M El Shwihdi

They decided that he had grown up. He was now a man with shoulders wider than those of his father. It would be a disgrace for him to remain without employment. They decided that he should discontinue his education at which he was a failure, and that he should follow the same path that all the boys in the neighbourhood had taken. He must start to build a life of his own and start to repay the debt he owed his parents. He himself felt that he had grown up and could see that his shoulders were wider than his father's. It irked him being without work and his father's careful ways with money annoyed him. He proclaimed a 'divorce' against his studies three times and proceeded to look for a job. Eventually he found a modest clerical post in a firm and was delighted to find a few 'dinars' in his pocket. He looked forward to repaying his debt to his parents.

His mother approached him one day and asked him to choose a wife from amongst the girls in the neighbourhood. He started to daydream as he stood upright in the middle of the lounge. He began to imagine his future lovely wife who would be shy of her shadow as it followed her on a sunny day, yet would not be coy enough that she would be unable to stand in his presence and converse with him, wearing a short modern dress. A wife with black eyes in whose depths his own eyes could swim effortlessly; but she would lower her glance modestly upon meeting the gaze of a stranger. A wife who possessed a fine lineage, high morals and a generous heart.

He moaned without uttering a word. His mother stood there unable to read his thoughts, feeling embarrassed as she waited for one word from him. His father, who was leaning on a cushion on a rush mat in the inner courtyard, also awaited that word.

Eventually he said:

'Choose a wife? Whoever God chooses and you approve of would be fine with me ...'

His mother smiled and insisted that he specify one particular girl, some girl whom he had admired maybe, and perhaps he had desired her to be his wife, but shyness had prevented him from declaring her identity. He remained silent as his mother stood there unable to understand him, and his father in the courtyard waiting.

He could imagine that future wife standing there smiling shyly and he returned her smile with an even broader one. His mother returned it with a fond mother's smile as she heard him whisper a name. The smile died on her lips. The girl's image disappeared from his mind and he felt his heart beating violently, anticipating a disaster.

His mother said:

'You know very well that she is from a rich family. You also know that she has gained her final certificate this year, which means, my son, that her dowry would not be less than 100 "dinars." Add to this other incidentals, the sum would rise to 2,000 "dinars" ... that's if her family consented ...'

He gulped, and was painfully aware of his situation, but he wanted to save his mother further hurt, so he smiled:

'They're all women ... no difference between this one and that one ... I was only teasing you when I chose the one I named. Didn't I tell you that whoever God chooses and you approve of would be fine with me?!'

His mother remained silent, to allow her son an opportunity for choice. In order that he should not run away with himself, she decided to talk to him in more detail and explain the situation:

'Now take the daughter of your 'Sayed' Mahmoud, Simha. By God, if you could only see her, you'd think the was a Christian – green eyes – long blonde hair – tall and in the bloom of youth! She has not been seen in the streets for ten years, ever since she was 7. It's true that her father has to work presently and that her family are not rich, also she is illiterate like me, but tell me, haven't I made a fine man out of you, as God willed? This one's dowry, my son, would not exceed 100 "dinars" ... and I think she would suit you ...

As for the daughter of 'Haj' Ali ... she is not illiterate, my son. She has attended school till the third elementary year. She is a pleasant, polite girl – apprehensive of her own shadow. She wears European clothes as if she was a European herself, nothing wrong with her, son, a well brought-up girl. Also your 'Sayed Haj' Ali is a good man. This one ... her dowry would not be more that 150 "dinars" ... she too could be your destiny ... haven't you seen her?

He felt that he should participate in the conversation, so he asked:

'What about Zahra?'

His mother appeared as if she had been stung by that name and hastily replied:

'God forbid, son! God forbid ...Zahra has no modesty ... she vainly saunters all day long wearing a short dress, swinging her handbag, in Thalam Market and in Omar Mukhtar Street, jostling with the men as if she was one herself, without embarrassment ... No, by God, my son .. haven't you heard all the stories about her?'

He smiled ... the old woman kept quiet for a moment then added:

'By God! That Zahra! ... if her hand were joined to mine, I would cut my hand off! As for her parents, in spite of their poverty, they behave above their station. Believe me, my son, despite all that is said about Zahra, they think she would get the same dowry as a respectable college girl, forgetting that this useless girl failed her primary certificate twice ...'

His father's impatient voice reached them from the courtyard, calling for his mother:

'Listen ... come here ...'

The old woman replied instantly:

'Patience ... Patience ...'

She started again listing the other offers, and was saved by a tempting offer which she preferred above the rest:

'Your 'Sayed' Suleiman's daughter ... Zainab ... you must have seen her from time to time ... what's your opinion of her?! Don't you think she's pretty, well-behaved and well-brought-up? By God, my son, she has plenty of suitors but they're all turned down because her father is looking for a decent man and not for a fortune. By God, my son, if we approached them they would not do us short ... any sensible man would wish you for his daughter.'

'How much is this one?'

She didn't understand .

'Yes?'

He replied:

'Her dowry ... how much is her dowry?'

The old woman started at the ceiling of the room then returned her gaze to her son:

'Zainab has attained the primary certificate ... her dowry ... let's say 200 "dinars," my son, maybe more but we shan't pay more than this because we cannot ...'

His father called his mother again. She excused herself, promising to return. He remained alone in the lounge. His mind's eye roamed over many girls, he settled on one of them who pleased him and he kept her image there until his mother returned. He whispered:

'Nouriyah ... Nouriyah, the daughter of my 'Sayed' Outhman .. what's your opinion of her?'

His mother groaned and was silent for a while. He asked her again about her opinion and she replied:

'This one, son, has gained her preparatory certificate. Her father hopes that she will become a teacher. Her dowry would not be less than 500 "dinars" plus overheads. We, my son, are poor. You are more aware and better informed of our situation than anyone else; but we're looking for a girl who would please you in spite of our budget. We are in a quandary about you and we ...'

She suddenly stopped, as if she regretted laying her cards on the table. Silence reigned totally over the room, several minutes passed slowly, until she decided that a choice must be made:

'Haven't you decided anything?'

He didn't answer, but kept staring at the floor with distracted eyes. She repeated her question but he didn't answer. She threw him the last tempting offer:

'The daughter of the new neighbours – tall and well-built with nice eyes, as full of youth as God wishes. She has been transferred to the second preparatory year but I hear that her uncle has forbidden her from finishing her education ... what's your opinion if we went ahead and asked for her hand?!'

He lifted his head up angrily:

'And how much does this one cost?!'

His mother asked:

'You mean her dowry? ... I can persuade her father that we pay them 250 "dinars" provided that they go easy on us with the rest of the conditions. You know how much the other overheads cost ... Oh, my son ... if ...'

He interrupted her angrily:

'Listen to me ... I shan't buy any of them ... I shall remain a bachelor until I can buy the merchandise that suits me, but for the time being I shan't buy ... no ...'

His mother left him to go and complain to his father. They had failed in making a choice.

11

The Mission
Yusef Guwairi

It felt heavy upon his back as he moved. It was so heavy, but the sand beneath him was soft and cold. The air stung his face and neck. A strange smell penetrated his nostrils. His ears were filled with a whispering sound.

It might have been the scent of the night mixed with those wild herbs as he pushed his body crawling on sand. Yet it might have been the odour of something else as he was not used to such a slow, crawling pace at night. The battles he used to wage were quick – blitzkrieg-like – on mountain steppes, slopes and in forests. This battle now was waging so tempestuously within him, yet it made no noise. He was entering the war all alone and ever so slowly; slithering along like a snake deliberately slowly and cautiously. Anything might happen at any moment now!

'I'll carry it ...'

'Imran?'

'Yes.'

Quick directions ensued. The officer patted him on the shoulder and his comrades were enthused. Something ponderous was weighted down between his shoulder-blades. Latifa's eyes glittered with emotion.

He remembers all that had taken place on the mountain and can well recall it clearly in the mind and yet it seems to be very remote. Only an hour ago the officer announced the mission. He volunteered:

'I'll carry it ...'

'Imran?' the officer asked.

'Yes,' he replied.

As he descended the bulge of the mountain making his way through ravines, the mission was secure on his back as well as in his heart and through every muscle and fibre of his being. He knew that his regiment would abandon the mountain for another place as soon as he reached his destination.

As he struggled down the mountain paths he encountered broad, flattened stones; rough sharp rocks; perilous, slippery slopes; and yet it felt no more than a resumption of his old, early battles. He was familiar with mountains. He loved them. He had waged many a lightning attack at their feet. A sense of preparedness and of verve began to rise in him dilating his nostrils. How he wished then to be able to leap on his enemy with a loud battle cry, calling his comrades as he showered terror from his automatic gun!

Imran passed his hand over his shoulder. He sensed the weight and pushed his fingers into the sand, tightening his fist on a handful of it.

His gun was there. He had never parted with it for a single moment before. It became a part of him – a strong, integral part that knew well how to speak to enemies decisively and fast! It was there. A new fighter will take it or they may use it to replace an old, faulty gun. How he wished to fall upon it now and hold it in his arms! He would then rise up thundering his battle cry, calling his comrades as he leapt like a panther with his gun chattering and resounding in the din of whistling bullets flying past!

He was overwhelmed with this sensation as he climbed down the mountain carrying his task on his back and leaving his regiment behind. He did not actually miss his gun as he climbed down the mountain. He was only convinced that once he reached the bottom of it and spotted a passing enemy he would perforate his body with holes.

'Our guns are truly ourselves.'

Latifa said these words to him as they were standing opposite one of the headquarters.

He was then holding his gun against his leg, busily cleaning and burnishing it.

'Our guns are truly ourselves.'

Still carrying on with the task in hand, he responded saying; 'But we are more than guns – we are strong. The guns are always in our hands.'

But now he does not know the secret of the new feeling which began to take hold of him. It was an odd sensation which crept in the moment he left the mountain without his gun. The mountain seemed now like a huge mass of darkness behind him, while there stretched before him an endless, soundless, flat surface of cold sand charged with a terrifying hush. It seemed like a whispering sound as he crawled across a sea of silence never casting a glance behind at the mountain where he had left his comrades.

One hour and a half had passed since he left, but time in his perception began to stretch and expand as though he was recalling memories mantled with the passage of many long years!

This inching along and the intimidation of what the darkness may hold in store as he stretched along the soft sand, pulling and releasing his body like a snake, filled him with apprehension. This dragging on held within its folds at every moment some cause for anxiety, for he was without his gun which he cherished more than his own limbs. He remembered the enthusiasm of his colleagues which so fired his mind and heart; the persistence with which Latifa's eyes shone, whose image was reflected on the face of every rock as he climbed down the mountain; and the big, rough, affectionate hand of his officer with a finger blown off in the war, patting his shoulder, communicating to him something bigger than could be expressed in words. But all of that was gone – nothing would be with him as he carried his weight to its destination. Amidst silence and apprehension he was carrying his mission all alone.

The night was thickening and Imran moved further and further into the desert. His hands were ever stretching forward and his feet pushing backwards in a slow, precise rhythm. The whispering sound in his ears grew louder emerging from what seemed to be an invisible source.

That thing secured on his back grew heavier as he crawled on. The weight intensified and pressed against him, making him feel as though he were carrying the bulk of the mountain, shifting its mass to some other place. This thought astounded him. Could he really lift a mountain? His colleagues were still on the summit and there he was carrying them all, together with his gun and Latifa. They were so near now. They were actually with him! How could he have left them elsewhere?...

...... Silence and the slow pace make him apprehensive? Was not the lofty earth on which his comrades stood and on whose rocks and slopes he fought so ferociously moving along with him? Surely he was carrying them all on his back. There's the affectionate hand with missing finger still patting his shoulder, expressing something stronger than any feeling and there too Latifa with her eyes ever twinkling before him. The enthusiasm of his colleagues was still kindling that flame in his heart and in place of one he now had a hundred guns!

His elbow hit a piece of stone which he pushed away. The sand was getting much colder. The stars were shining with a dim light. Imran suddenly realised that the sand beneath him began to vanish and in its place short shrubs were hitting against his body. He knew that he must be approaching his target.

He could not distinguish anything in the distance but he froze for a moment and pushed his body flat against the earth burying his head in the grass. Powerful floodlights like betraying eyes were intermittently and surreptitiously scanning the area ever so slowly revealing, as they cast their beams across the distance, a fence of barbed wire. Fluttering shadows of the shaken barbed wire began to form against the grass. As the light scanned the distance the shadows floated menacingly like impending death! It was death!

Imran held his breath and pressed his body further and further into the grass as though he had become rooted to the ground.

The light from the tall tower was drawing an arc from left to right. Imran could hear its sound like the rustle of leaves – like the blade of a sharp knife drawn against him. He sank more closely to the earth. He had not yet approached the fence of barbed wire, but the searchlight was throwing its rays further that the perimeter of the fence.

The light drew nearer and nearer until it reached Imran himself. He felt its rays pressing against his back so heavily. It was more ponderous than any mountain. It was crushing his ribs and ripping his back in two. At that moment as he embraced death there were unleashed in him fears and strange perceptions which he had never seen so clearly before.

As the rays of light lingered about him, he became tense. He tasted fear for the first time. He had not known fear before. It was sweeping through him like a mighty torrent crushing him to bits and making his heart shrink. Then all of a sudden the shadow of night descended once more. The lethal shaft of light had moved away casting slowly moving shadows of vibrating wires against the grass. It kept on receding in to the distance until silence prevailed. It was a 'rustling' silence in the wake of the light which had vanished as suddenly as it had appeared.

Imran lifted his head and began to move his body along the grass. The experience had made him giddy.

How and why was he afraid? In the darkness a smile of recognition began to break over his lips. 'I know the reason!' he thought. He felt light and agile. The battle cry was gathering momentum in his heart as he proceeded to crawl.

He was afraid to die. He was perturbed as the prospect of certain death took him unawares.

But had he not chosen that fate himself? Was it not he who had planned it all? Surely he had not left the mountain top with that heavy burden on his back without expecting to face death! He had volunteered for it for the sake of the mission.

The fear which gripped him was not for his own fate but rather lest he should fail to fulfil his duty. Should he meet death before its accomplishment his volunteering will have been futile.

'I'll carry it.'

'Imran?'

'Yes.'

It was still against his shoulder but it did not feel heavy any more. It was as light as a feather. The heaviness he had felt as he crawled on the sand was the weight of fear. Something might have sprung on him from out of the folds of darkness to end his journey at an earlier stage.

The journey as he had planned it was nearing its end. His target in the form of a dark building stood only feet away. He moved in between the barbed wire with agility and speed. A steel spike ripped open his cheek but he did not feel the cut. He was stronger than steel and its hidden spikes; mightier than the dark building; more powerful than anything he could think of. An extraordinary strength swept through him empowering his arms and erupting in his whole body like a volcano.

'Our guns are truly ourselves.'

'But we are more than mere guns. We are stronger.'

Latifa was now approaching him – growing larger and larger – carrying in her hands a cluster of shimmering stars which she scattered on his shoulders. The affectionate, rough palm of the officer grew in size until it filled the horizon waving and greeting him. The enthusiasm of his friends was now illuminating the sky above and the earth below.

'We are stronger.'

Imran was no longer aware of himself. He was only conscious that the feeling of loneliness had slipped away giving rise to a new sensation.

'We ...'

Indeed it was the spirit of Algiers! It was the mountains and the dales and the wilderness and the people and the hundreds of children, all with eyes like Latifa's. Latifa may die too. So may thousands of others – but the homeland will remain.

His veins swelled as he nimbly undid the huge bundle fixed on his back. He was quick as a bullet. He got ready and then glanced at the gate of the French station. A dim shaft of light was streaming from inside breaking its beams against the stony threshold. The footsteps of heavy boots clattered in the distance.

Imran struck a match. His taut, glowing features were lit. The

flame moved slowly towards the bundle and when the wick caught
fire Imran embraced the bundle tightly to his chest. He lifted his
head and gave a resounding cry which echoed through the walls as
he dashed through the gate.

In his mind the thought, 'They are waiting at the mountain top,'
kindled his violent wrath.

A few fearful moments passed.

Then the explosion reverberated like rolling thunder.

12

The Last Station
Ahmed Ibrahim al Fagih

No sooner had I opened the door and saw her sitting near the window – as a waft of her perfume hit me in the face – then my head was filled with the strains of some demented feverish music, performed by a band whose musicians excelled in beating the drums with their heads and the heels of their shoes, and a guitarist who almost bit the strings and strummed them with his teeth, and howled his song. I stood at the door for an instant to regain my breath and remove the strain from my arm after carrying my suitcase. The woman raised her eyes towards me and in a corner of my memory nightclub lights flashed, the sort which blinked on and off in the fashion of fire engines, ambulances and police cars; and where the dancers underneath those lights gyrated hysterically as if worshipping a God of violence, sex and crime.

I asked her permission to sit down and she nodded her head. In my mind there stirred images from spy thriller reels, scenes which alternated from police chases to torrid love adventures. Something about this woman exuded stimulation, seduction and sex appeal. She sat quietly in her seat, attentively reading a large book spread over her knees, and wearing eye glasses, for she had probably strained her eyesight in too much studying and reading.

She wore a grey jacket and had folded a long scarf several times round her neck. It appeared that she had made a fine art out of camouflage on this autumn day which had borrowed something from winter days. Yet in spite of all this protection she had the kind of beauty which would still proclaim itself no matter how well hidden. Hers was an aggressive beauty, like a tiger which is unleashed to devour you as soon as you approach; but it became apparent to me that she was greatly embarrassed by this beauty, with its violent, ferocious and torrid quality.

She wore her glasses and all those clothes and placed the largest books possible on her lap in a desperate effort to stem the rebelliousness of that unruly beauty. She even declined from wearing even a hint of lipstick or emollient so that her lips appeared parched and dry. She had bound her well-endowed and thrusting breasts within the most sedate and severe clothes, imprisoning them so cruelly. She chose the dullest shade of grey and bought a scarf at least a hundred feet long to rap round her neck to prevent even a glimmer of smooth marble-like neck from peeping out or twinkling through. As for those eyes with the thick long lashes which sent out flashes like the guns used by aliens from the other planets in science fiction films, with the power to smite and destroy, she had tried to remedy the situation by wearing her glasses, which she now uses for reading. One can sense from the first instant that she took great pains to conceal her beauty or at least to subdue and submerge it; for no doubt it had caused her a great deal of annoyance at every stage of her life. She had not been able to live anywhere without fights breaking out amongst the young men in the neighbourhood because of her. She had not been able to go out into the street without attracting a crowd, which in turn drew the attention of the keepers of law and order. She had not been able to enter a restaurant, or a place of public entertainment, or a shop or business premises without people neglecting their business to stare at her. Perhaps she had grown accustomed to this reaction and had reached a high standard of controlling her beauty, and taming its wildness. That's how she was able to walk down the street, and enter a restaurant or a place of entertainment and avoid all these demonstrations and rivalry. She had succeeded in keeping the tigers within her safely locked away in their cages and that's why she now sat calmly in her seat, unaware that those tigers only needed a tourist from an Eastern country like me, with a longing for life, to cause them to bound out of their cages, smashing their chains and breaking the locks to sink their claws and teeth into his flesh.

The thick fog outside was pressing like a pack of hyenas a few metres away from the station. I had sprawled on the opposite seat next to the door and wished I had the courage to sit next to her or directly opposite. This would facilitate the opportunity of striking up a conversation with her, but what could I do to change a shy nature that had been my lot all my life? It was brave enough of me to sit in a compartment alone with her at all, and not run away because of embarrassment, which her beauty was arousing in me. I thanked God that the train had moved before other passengers had the chance to occupy the seats which separated us. I didn't have the time to buy a newspaper or a magazine with which to occupy myself during the journey. I barely managed to catch the train at the last minute. She was content to read her book and had no need to turn to something else to pass the time, such as entering into a casual conversation with an unknown companion on the journey. She didn't lift her head off the book, for she had used it as a barricade to discourage any intruders from approaching the gardens of her palace.

I started to invent reasons to justify my failure to strike up a conversation with her. I pretended that I would have succeeded with this woman if only I could have met her on her own without that accursed book. I watched the trees flashing past, and the fields which stretched far into the distance, shrouded in the morning mist and managed to pass the time by reading the book of nature. I started to invest the shapes outside covered by the mist with other meanings, imagining that some were tents, while others looked like riders wearing white-clothes, mounting white horses and stirring up clouds of dust around them, but suddenly nature disappeared.

The train entered a tunnel and I noticed that inside the compartment pale yellow lights became visible in the gloom. Their effect transformed the woman into what painters must have imagined the Virgin Mary to look like. I saw her suddenly acquire a saintly glow which endowed her with a calm strange beauty. She appeared as if she did not belong to this world. She was a saint reading her bible and intoning her prayers in a deserted temple high up on a mountain top, kneeling there at dawn and worshipping alone in the lamplight

We emerged from the tunnel and the holy mantle slipped off. Once more the rowdy music started to flow from her breasts, her lips and her eyes. The reels of sex and violence once again emerged from the blonde hair cascading over her shoulders; the car chases and the fire engine flowed from the pages of the book spread over her knees. I instantly pictured her with various lovers and presumed that she was on her way back from visiting the one in the country, who had bought her a mansion there. She was now going to her lover who lived in the city. He had moved to live in with her after divorcing his wife and abandoning his children and quitting his job. She would then kick him out after squandering all his money.

There was also the student whom she had enticed away from his studies and who now made ends meet hanging round bars and night spots. The fourth, fifth or sixth who had spent all his money on her, even to the extent of selling his business and closing up shop or firm, had gone bankrupt.

The seventh or eighth had lost his job or his mind. She also had relationships with some politicians, in the event of one of them becoming a minister of state; but a rival for this lovely lady's affections was the chief editor of a national newspaper who had discovered a scandal concerning the minister and had exposed him.

This had caused a sensation in political circles which led to the downfall of the government and the current party in power was out of favour, having lost the confidence of the nation. She had now got rid of all her previous lovers and kept only one. I imagined him to be, in order to control her seductive powers, a very tough and cruel man with a powerful build. I chose for him a violent profession. In spite of losing the sight of one eye, he was the second-in-command of a large gang engaged in smuggling and drugs. I wanted him to be the second-in-command of the organisation because he would have to be the man of action, entrusted with the job of carrying things out. The top man always planned and organised. I didn't want him to be the brains, but merely the steel arm manipulated by the brains. I didn't mind reserving a place for him near the top of the ladder of success to which he aspired. His ambition would reveal other ugly aspects of his nature when a rival gang would use him to plot the elimination of his boss; who was his benefactor and who had helped him and promoted him to his present position in the organisation.

I mused to myself that it was a great shame that she got herself involved in a relationship with the one-eyed man. Suffice it the wide age gap between them – for in spite of his powerfully large frame and a health as strong as an ox – he was approaching 50 while she was merely 21 or 22. I wished he could have valued that beauty, but even if he did appreciate it, he only persisted in vanquishing and humiliating it. He saw himself as an opponent in a battle in which his ugliness and uncouthness (his face was full of warts and he had a flat shaped bald head), would triumph over the charms of this woman, her allure and her bewitching beauty which shone from her eyes, her hair, her neck, her brow, her breasts and her lips. He realised that should he weaken, his defeat would be assured and he would lose that enchanting female forever. He had triumphed over her because from the very beginning he had treated her with viciousness, as if avenging all the ugly faces in the world against this woman who was the symbol of beauty, and who suffered on behalf of all the beautiful creatures on the face of this earth. He had discovered in treating her thus a new aspect to his personality, an agreeable and pleasing feeling, and he derived pleasure from hurting and humiliating her.

Whenever he desired her, he savagely tore the clothes off her, ripping them with his nails, piece by piece, until she was completely naked. I had guessed from his coarse features that he was not merely content with hitting her with his hands or kicking her with his feet, but that he used chairs, dishes, pieces of furniture and even kitchen utensils against her as a punishment, whenever she raised her voice at him. Despite her present demeanour which conveyed a regal dignity, I knew how she suffered and screamed as she knelt at his feet, weeping and begging for mercy and pity. This only increased his violence and his desire to humiliate and torment her. Afterwards he took her almost by force. I noticed a small scratch on her left temple which confirmed all my suspicions. I was certain that his fingernails had left their mark on her face. She was obviously trying to cover the traces beneath her hair and was using the heavy scarf to conceal the bruises which her neck had sustained as a result of his sadistic treatment.

The image of horses conjured up by the fog dissipated as the morning sun bathed the green fields which stretched as far as the horizon. The world appeared beautiful and cheerful. I realised that I was falling irresistibly in love with this woman whose delicious mouth burst with forbidden desires. She lifted her head off the pages of the book and her eyes swept across the floor of the compartment and came to rest on my face for a few seconds, as if she had just discovered my presence. I felt a tremor run through me, as if I had crept stealthily into a queen's bedchamber, who would then call the guards and have me killed. I dropped my gaze to the floor so our eyes would not meet, for fear that she might discover the thoughts which ran in my mind. She returned to her book, after she had excused and forgiven me. I felt remorseful for filling her life with all that terror and for having firmly secured its chains around her, like the three lower circles in Dante's hell. I thanked God that our thoughts had no voice, otherwise she would have screamed for help after discovering what I had been secretly thinking about her. If I was brave I could have approached her with a pleasant remark about the beauty of the morning. The shyness which had been my companion all my life prevented me from making the first move. I made a resolution that I would stop myself falling in love with all women, until I found an exceptionally attractive woman who would strike up a conversation with me first! I would devote all my love to her! Still I remembered that there was an ogre in the life of this female, who laid siege around her and prevented her from addressing strangers. The shadow of the ugly man followed her everywhere she went. He watched all her looks, her words and her movements. I was certain that he had her followed and that someone was spying on us this very minute through a chink in the door. The poor wretch could not escape his clutches, for he had threatened her with death should she even contemplate leaving him. Yet there must be a way of saving her. Why didn't she leave him and escape to a distant country and put an end to this existence, filled with violence and misery? There was the problem of where she could find the money to enable her afford the costs of the journey and settling down somewhere. She was of humble origins and her family were so poor they were reduced to begging. Her mother could not afford any medications and had died from a fever. Her father was taken to an old people's home. Her aunt lived in the country and that awful man did not allow her to visit except once or twice a year. The aunt lived alone and depended on some aid from her niece. She was probably back on her way from a short visit now. She had saved every extra penny she had to help out her aunt. What a noble character!

I was filled with pain, thinking of a way to save her from all this misery. I watched her as she read her book, exuding her magic in dignity and silence. My love for her increased and I wished that she was indeed a queen and I was her secret lover, visiting her furtively and enfolding her royal body tenderly. That body which was like a richly laden table, brimming with delicacies, strolling across its gardens filled with blooms, then ascending to its high balconies, picking what I fancied from its abundance of apples, grapes or pomegranates, and drinking from its mature vintage wines. In the midst of my ecstasy at possessing this body through whose veins blue blood ran, a thought struck me. Why didn't she inform the police about him?!

That was her only way out to free herself from his clutches and end her years of misery, spent in his company. He would be thrown behind bars and would not be released from a gloomy prison until he was a very old man.

Don't worry about what would happen to you afterwards. I shall hasten to your side. I shall labour and suffer to make you happy. Oh delight of my heart, I shall be your obedient servant worshipping at your altar. I shall help your beauty regain its respect and shall offer you such love as no man has given a woman before me. I had been looking at her, glad that the time was approaching to save her, but for some reason, I saw her throw the book she held between her hands to the floor. She leapt up, anger consuming her brow and her face darkened with a strange sorrow as if she had seen the most horrible and awful vision. She rapidly advanced towards me. I rose from my seat and looked at her with astonishment. I saw her hand rise and I felt the sting of a violent slap across my face, as if I had committed the most heinous crime against her!

'You scoundrel!'

I was so taken aback, I didn't know what to do and remained standing there speechless. I hadn't been sitting close enough so that any movement on my part could have justified a mistaken interpretation. I tried to say something but I heard her shouting at me, tears stinging her eyes:

'What business is it of you to entertain such sick thoughts about saving me? Who gave you the right to interfere in my affairs or act on my behalf? It's my life and I am free to do whatever I like with it.

I remained transfixed in my spot, overwhelmed with confusion and shock. I was transformed into a statue made of clay or wood, unable to comprehend or act or reason or see or hear or speak. I didn't know how much time elapsed while in this state. When life began to return to my wooden frame I felt the floor of the compartment shudder underneath my feet. I realised the train had put on its brakes and it reached the last station. A porter opened the door of the carriage and asked us to get ready to leave the train. He saw me standing there looking bewildered and saw her sitting there crying. He looked at me curiously and asked her what had happened, but she didn't reply. She collected her bags and hastily departed. The porter thought I was her companion and said with a smile :

'Don't worry about it! Tiffs will happen between lovers!'

I saw him standing there on the platform through the window. He was an immense giant of about fifty. His head was flat shaped and bald. His face was full of warts. One eye was covered by a patch, the other eye was expectantly looking at those descending the train.